LATIGO'S CHANCE

ALSO BY PATRICK LINDSAY

Opening the Frontier: Spencer and Son

Latigo Series

Latigo's Choice: Taming the West

LATIGO'S CHANCE

BOOMTOWN GOLD

LATIGO BOOK TWO

PATRICK LINDSAY

WOLFPACK
PUBLISHING
— EST 2013 —

Latigo's Chance: Boomtown Gold
Paperback Edition
Copyright © 2024 Patrick Lindsay

Wolfpack Publishing
1707 E. Diana Street
Tampa, FL 33610

wolfpackpublishing.com

Paperback ISBN 978-1-63977-654-2
eBook ISBN 978-1-63977-653-5
LCCN 2024945511

LATIGO'S CHANCE

ONE
BOOMTOWN

SILVERTON, COLORADO—1879

We had a bull, back when I was a boy, that went by the name of Shorty. He was a peaceful, nice bull most of the time, but once in a while, he got a notion to give me some trouble. My pa used to say that Shorty was pure ornery when he got him one of those notions. Pa was right about most things.

When Shorty got him a notion, he lowered that gigantic head of his and took to pawin' the ground with his front feet. I knew I had to check for the fastest way out of the pasture, or the corral, or what-have-you when he commenced to pawin' like that.

The thing is, I knew I had to pick up my big feet and make some tracks for sure if Shorty did that thing with his eyes. He was a little cross-eyed, Shorty was, so he wasn't a looker, as my granny would say. Sometimes she would say I'm a looker, but her eyesight wasn't so good when she got older.

Anyway, Shorty would narrow down those eyes and get all squinty-like, then he'd paw the ground one more time, let out a beller, and charge. I'm here to tell you, you'd best have cleared out of his way when that happened. Shorty could move right along when he set his mind to it.

I was thinkin' about ol' Shorty when I had to tell this old miner named Buford that we had cut his beer off for the rest of the night. Buford could hold his beer real good until he couldn't, if you know what I mean. He got real touchy an' started to growl and rumble when you cut off his beer. And that was usually just the first part. I knew what came next.

Buford climbed down off his stool and glared at me when I told him he was done for the night. He'd started some caterwauling he called singin', and it was driving folks out of the saloon. That and he'd spilled his last beer on the customer next to him. I told him he had to make tracks out of the Suds 'n Such Saloon. Buford looked over at my partner, Holt, back behind the bar. Holt crossed his arms and shook his head at Buford.

Buford turned around to glare at me again. I backed off just a smidge to give him some room to get around me on the way out. He started to rumbling. I took a quick look at his feet just to make sure he wasn't pawin' the ground, but he didn't do that part the same as Shorty.

That was when I saw it, though, right when I looked back up. He narrowed those eyes and looked at me all squinty-like, just like Shorty. I braced myself just as he let out a beller and charged at me. He was stumblin' a little, but he had a good head of steam and I couldn't wait around to get plowed into the wall.

I dodged just as he got to me and gave him a good shove as he stumbled past. I might have hauled off and landed a haymaker in his belly, but he'd had a lot of beer, and I was a little afraid of what might happen if I busted him in the belly.

Buford came up short against the wall when he hit it with a crash. Then he gathered himself together and turned around for another run at me. He looked a little pale around the gills this time. That crash into the wall must have stung a little. He came at me and swung a big right hand and missed. I grabbed a handful of his hair and yanked it until he squawked. His eyes started to water.

"We're goin' outside now, Buford," I told him. "You're gonna go back to your room at the boarding house an' sleep it off. You can have some more beer tomorrow."

Well, he kinda nodded, so I thought things were all good now. I kept ahold of his hair, though, just in case, walked him over to the doors, and shoved him out to the street. I dusted my hands off, walked backed into the saloon, and took maybe three or four steps when Holt, my partner, pointed and shouted.

"Behind you, Lat!"

I heard him comin' at me now, building up a lot of speed like a big train. I spun around, and then I saw one of the dangdest things I ever saw.

A grizzled old fella, maybe late fifty-somethin' and not very big, hopped off a stool at the end of the bar and stepped out in front of that moving freight train.

He grabbed Buford by the thumb on one of those big paws of his and twisted that thumb around until ol' Buford screeched and went to his knees.

Buford clawed the air and swung, trying to get at that old grizzled guy, but he couldn't reach him. The guy took up the twist on his thumb by another notch, and Buford collapsed flat on the floor. He just lay there and moaned. Then the guy started talkin', and never even raised his voice a notch.

"They done taken you outta here nice one time, Buford," he explained. "And you got all rowdy and come back to make trouble. Well, Buford, this here is as nice as I'm gonna treat you. I feel like a man should have a chance, though, so I'm gonna let go of your thumb so you can go back out all quiet-like."

Buford mumbled something. He might have been nodding his head, but I couldn't tell.

"The thing is, though, Buford," the guy said. "If'n you come back in here all rowdy again, I'm likely to get riled a bit myself, and you don't want me to get riled. Okay?"

Buford mumbled again, and the guy let go of his thumb. Buford got up, dusted himself off, glared at me one more time, then went out the door as peaceful as a lamb.

Holt came around the bar, pointing at me and laughing. "Yore chin's hangin' down, pard," he said. "I think you're plumb surprised. You told me to find somebody else to throw out the rowdies around here, so I done it. Meet Sarge."

I turned around and stared at the grizzled old guy who just made Buford as peaceful as a kid in Sunday

School. Well, I wasn't ever that peaceful in Sunday School, myself, but Buford was acting like the good kids in my class.

Let me tell you a little about myself. My name is Latigo Smith. I stand about six foot one and go about one hundred ninety pounds. When Sarge came over to me, I'm guessin' he's about five foot nine and one-sixty, soaking wet, as they say.

Sarge chuckled and shook my hand. "You settled him down some," Sarge said. "I jest had to explain things a little more to him."

I grinned and pushed a beer in Sarge's direction. "Where did you learn to do that?" I asked. "That was some mighty fine explaining."

Sarge took a long slurp. The beer was half gone when he set it back down. He squinted at the ceiling. "Well, now, let's see... I was in the army for a while durin' the war. Did some mining, ranch foreman for a while, did some sheriffing. Picked up a little bit every-where, I guess. I had to do some explaining in most of them jobs."

I shook my head while Holt clapped me on the back. "I hired Sarge today," Holt crowed. "You can just pop in for a beer ever' now and then and help me out with the bar. Collect your twenty percent of profits on your money, like we agreed. Sarge can throw 'em out when he needs to."

I went to get myself a beer to replace the one I'd given to Sarge. I glanced over my shoulder as I walked away. "Sarge," I said, "you seem like a downright useful man to know. Maybe I can get you to help once in a while if I get myself in a tight spot."

Sarge sucked down the last of the beer and waved his empty glass in the air. "You got it," he told me.

Since Holt didn't need any help inside, I moved out and took a seat on a bench. I could see Buford weaving his way down the street, sucking on his thumb and probably trying to figure out how a guy half his size just did that to him. I grinned when I thought about it.

I was happy that Holt had found somebody to help him out in the saloon. Silverton, Colorado, was a pretty new town, but there were lots of miners, which meant he had lots of customers. He had mostly needed help keeping things under control.

I had invested some of the money that my girl Joanna and I had made when we made a gold strike out on the Animas River. Well, it was kind of a gold strike. Her granddaddy and my uncle had found gold inside some black rocks years before. Something about iron in the riverbank and running water and the rocks took on a black look. Anyway, Joanna and I had found more of 'em just a little while back.

So, I had bought twenty percent of Holt's new saloon when we all moved to Silverton. Holt had invested most of his money and he ran the saloon full time, so he got the rest of the profits. That suited me just fine. I liked a good saloon, but I didn't want to spend all my time in it.

Joanna had just opened herself a new bakery in town, and that was doing great, too. Miners and a few cowboys around here liked bread and cakes and such just about as much as they liked saloons.

That brought me around to wondering what I was going to do for myself. I'd been a railroad security man—well, actually, I ran the construction of the railroad for a while. Mostly, I just let other folks do their jobs and busted some heads when they needed it.

I'd been a deputy sheriff in Texas for a while, too. Before that, I'd done a little ranching and a little mining. My girl Joanna thinks I should start a ranch up here in the high country, raise a little beef, and grow some hay I could ship out on the new railroad. I'm still thinking about that one. I've probably got enough money to do it, though.

I heard a ruckus goin' on inside and turned to see a guy coming out of the saloon, but he wasn't none too happy about it. Sarge had ahold of his ear and was pulling him right through the doors. This guy didn't sound any happier about things than Buford had. I chuckled and got up to head for the bakery. I was gonna have to steal this Sarge guy from Holt if I started a ranch up here. That man had him some skills.

———

The bakery building had gone up in a hurry. The inside wasn't done yet, but it had four walls, a roof, and a brick oven cranking out goods. She planned to call it just *Joanna's*. The sign painter had some work to do yet, so, for now, it just said *Joa*. The smells coming from inside were probably all she needed anyway. The miners started lining up outside before she opened at seven o'clock every morning.

A friend of hers from Durango had come over to help Joanna get started, but her friend, named Ma, had gone back home now, so Joanna had some really long days until she could afford to get some help. I knew she would have just finished cleaning up and preparing some dough for tomorrow.

I reached the front of the bakery just in time to hear the door open. Joanna stepped out, locked the door behind her, and leaned in to give me a kiss. She slipped her arm through mine, and we started walking to the boarding house where she had taken a room in town.

We sat down outside the place and I told Joanna about this new guy, Sarge. Holt had found to help him in the bar. When I finished with the story about the tough old miner getting hauled out by his ear, she was laughing so hard I saw a tear or two running down her cheek.

"If I get a ranch up here somewhere, I got to get Sarge to work for me," I told her. "He's been a ranch foreman and a lawman and been in the army, and I don't know what else."

She stopped laughing after a while and leaned in. "What about a ranch?" she asked. "Have you looked at any properties?"

"I've looked around," I said slowly. "And I've done some asking. Not about any land in particular, but I've been tryin' to get a feel for the area—costs and how folks are doing with ranching and growing hay up here."

"What'd you find out?" It surprised me how curious she was about this.

"Land's not too expensive so far," I answered. "With people flowing in here on the railroad for the mining, I expect it'll drive up prices after a while. The main thing is about the altitude. We're up over eight thousand feet, even if I ride south for a bit out of town. That makes for a pretty short growing season."

She sounded disappointed, so I hurried up to give her some good news. "Good land, though," I added. "And the railroads coming in will make it a lot easier and cheaper to get to market."

"Okay." She brightened up.

"I might have to do some irrigating, though," I finished. "If we have a dry year around here, there might not be enough water for the hay. Enough for cattle, but of course, the cattle need hay. I might have to do me some digging to get water to the hay."

"You could do that, though, right?" she persisted.

"I could," I agreed. "I would just have to get me a shovel and put it to work. Mebbe I could afford to hire a couple guys for a while to help. Maybe I could do it with a plow."

It got quiet for a while, then she seemed to remember something else she wanted to ask. "You haven't looked at any properties in particular, you said? Nothing you might want to put an offer on?"

"Not yet," I hedged. "I'll look around a little more, then maybe I could ask at the bank for anything they know about." I paused for a minute, not sure I wanted to tell her the next part. "Somebody said something at the saloon that I thought was a little strange."

I glanced sideways. She was locked in on me, just waiting.

"Somebody said they thought folks were getting discouraged from buying right now. I pressed him pretty hard for what he meant, but he just locked up and wouldn't say anything else. Don't know what he meant."

"Huh." She rested her head on my shoulder. I guess she was trying to make sense of that one, too.

After a minute or two, she squeezed my hand and pointed down the street. "New mayor is coming," she whispered. "Just got elected a few weeks ago. Mayor Knowles. He's been into the bakery a few times. Word is he's trying to get a sheriff appointed."

"Not interested," I growled.

She chuckled and squeezed my hand again. "I know," she murmured, "but somebody in the bakery gave him your name and said you'd been a deputy in Texas. I'll bet he asks you."

"Humph." I said nothing else and waited while he walked over to us.

Knowles tipped his hat at Joanna when he reached us. "Miss Joanna," he said, "is this your fella?"

Joanna introduced us. He grabbed my hand but looked at me a little sideways, I thought.

"Latigo," he said, drawin' out the name. "What do you think you'll do around this town?"

"I'm helping Joanna get the bakery started," I answered. "Also, I'm part owner of the Suds 'n Such Saloon down the street."

His eyebrows climbed up a little at that last part.

He stared down toward the saloon, stared back at me, opened his mouth like he wanted to say something, then changed his mind. He shuffled his feet a couple times, tipped his hat at Joanna, then left.

I watched him walk away, then looked over at Joanna. "That strike you kinda funny?" I asked. "He didn't know what to say when I said I'm part owner at the Suds 'n Such." I kept watching until he disappeared into the diner.

"That was...strange," she said. "He's always been all charm and personality in the diner, likes he's still working for votes. I don't know why he'd be so surprised about you owning the saloon with Holt. You're down there all the time. He'd probably seen you going in there."

I grinned. "Maybe Sarge threw him out a time or two."

She laughed, then thought for a minute. "You didn't say anything about looking for a ranch, did you?"

"Nope." I scratched my chin, shrugged, and stood up. "I decided not to tell him anything else he didn't need to know."

I kissed Joanna goodnight at the door to the boarding house and moved on down to the only hotel in town where I'd been staying since I got here. Part way there, it dawned on me I'd said nothing about my past as a deputy sheriff. Joanna said he knew about that. Maybe, I thought, he's already got somebody good in mind for the sheriff.

I didn't want that job, anyway. It was decent work

and all that, but what I really needed was a chance to make some good money in this new town. I figured it was time to find that chance.

TWO
SALOON STANDOFF

Cleo Ward pushed open the door of the railroad office in Durango and let it slam behind him. He thought of it as the railroad shack, not the office, but it served the purpose. Now that the line was complete, running all the way north to Silverton, things were a lot quieter. Quieter was true for now, but he wasn't convinced things would stay that way. As the general manager in charge of expansion for the Denver and Rio Grande Railroad, that had him a little worried.

Old habits started him down the street toward Ma's Bakery. Word had it that Ma was back from Silverton, and her place was open again. Cleo much preferred the food and coffee at Ma's, even though his friends Latigo and Joanna had moved on to Silverton.

Ward wiped his boots on the mat outside the bakery and heard the pleasant little bell ringing as he entered. It was pretty late for the breakfast crowd, but he liked it when things were quiet. He could see he had the place to himself. Ma hustled out from the back, making a fuss over him as usual and herding him to a table by the window. A new girl came over with the coffeepot to get him started.

Ward sat back with his coffee and stared out the window, enjoying the morning quiet. His railroad, the Denver and Rio Grande, had completed the narrow-gauge track from here in Durango out to Silverton. Ore and samples were flowing already from the rich deposits around Silverton. That was a victory. He could feel good about that.

What had him worried was the bitterness and bad blood between his railroad and the Santa Fe railroad. The two railroads had fought bitterly for the rights to build a line through The Royal Gorge, a critical pass through the mountains. The Denver and Rio Grande had won out in court, ending that problem for now. The Santa Fe was a powerful competitor, though, and had pretty much cut off Ward's railroad from connecting Denver with Santa Fe and points south and west. The D&RG, as it was called, would have to settle for building straight out west toward Utah. Still, the business from all the mining in the Colorado mountains was brisk.

Ward's thoughts were interrupted when Ma sat down in a chair across the table from him. She pushed a pastry over to him and smiled when he reached for it.

"On the house," she grinned. She studied his face. "Troubles?"

He immediately forced a smile to his face and took

a bite of the pastry. "Nothing I can't handle," he assured her.

"Uh-huh," said Ma, clearly unconvinced.

Ward chewed absently on the pastry for a moment, then took another swig of his coffee. Ma was seeing right through him, he thought uncomfortably.

He set the pastry back on the plate. "You just got back from Silverton, right?" he asked.

Ma nodded and waited.

Ward stalled behind another sip of coffee. "How are Joanna and Latigo doing?" he asked. Then, getting more to the point, he asked, "What is Lat up to?"

Ma smiled and stood. "They're doin' fine," she said, sending a knowing look in Ward's direction. "Lat don't seem to be doin' a whole lot yet. Maybe you could take a ride over there and see him."

Ward chuckled, left some money on the table, and left. That, he thought, sounded like a pretty good idea. He was worried more for his old friends, Latigo and Joanna, than he was for himself. There was a lot of news reaching his ears about some of the old railroad gunhands getting into the mining business being done up near Silverton, and not in a good way.

Boom towns always had plenty of trouble, and Ward didn't worry about Lat taking care of himself in ordinary boomtown situations like those. He'd heard things, though, that had him worried about his old friend. Latigo didn't back down from trouble—that was good. Maybe, though, Ward thought, he needed to make a trip and give his friend a heads-up about what he'd heard. A man always needed to be prepared.

Ward pulled his watch from his pocket and checked the time. He had a half hour to catch the train to Silverton. He walked slowly toward the new station.

———

I dropped into Holt's Suds 'n Such Saloon before the crowd showed up, looking for Sarge. I knew he'd been in this area for a while, and I wanted to sound him out on buying property around here. This was a mining town, after all, and there were lots of folks looking to separate a tinhorn from his money. I didn't plan on being one of those tinhorns.

I found him mopping up a beer spill in the corner. I offered to buy him a round. He just grinned and shook his head. "Kinda early for me to get started," he told me. "Got to have my head straight and the old reflexes workin' to throw out some of these guys." He stopped and thought for a second. "Mebbe just one," he decided.

Sarge motioned me over to a table in the corner. "What kin I do fer ya?" he asked.

"Looking to buy some land," I answered as Holt set down a pitcher and a couple of glasses. "High country grazing and hay crop."

Sarge nodded and poured us a glass apiece. "How many acres you thinkin' about?" he asked.

I squinted out the window. "Might depend on the price," I said, still staring out the window. "Maybe a hundred seventy-five or two hundred if I can cover it with cash. Maybe I can spread out a little from there."

Sarge chuckled. "Yeah," he said, "I heard about them black rocks you and Joanna found." He was talking about the gold find we'd made the year before in the Animas River near Durango. He took a turn staring out the window.

"Two ways you could go about it," he finally answered. "You ever heard tell of the Homestead Act?"

I nodded my head slowly. "Heard of it, don't know too much," I said. "Government law about home-steading on open land for free, or something like that."

"Yeah," Sarge nodded. "Not much free land left around here, though. You'll probly have to pay to get something you want. So," he continued, "you could ride around and see if'n you see anything you like. If you see a spot with no cattle grazin' and no crops this time of year, could be it's up for sale. Or, you could be lucky enough to see some folks movin' out. Some are doing that, I've heard tell."

"Yeah, I figgered on some of that," I agreed. "What about banks? Have they got any land for sale?"

"Possible," he allowed. "More likely to find some if you go see a land agent. We got one, just down the street a couple doors. Name of Aaron Budge." He opened his mouth like he was gonna say something else, then stopped and went back to staring out the window.

"What?" I pressed. "What are you not telling me?"

Sarge glanced over at me, then looked around the room. "Word has it," he muttered, "that the land agent in town don't seem to come up with much property except for buddies and other folks he wants to help. Everybody else don't seem to get any help from him."

"Hmmm." I took a pull on my beer and set it back down. "Who are these buddies he finds land for?"

Sarge looked around again and lowered his voice a little more. "Word is, the mayor's been gettin' hisself some right nice land," he mumbled. "Also, a feller that wears a couple tied-down guns and shows up here in the bar sometimes. Word is he mebbe worked for one of the railroads a while back."

I stared at Sarge. "What's this guy's name?" I asked. "Is he good with those guns, or is he just a show pony?"

Sarge scowled and buried his mug in his beer for a minute. "Dunno if he's good," he admitted. "I ain't interested in callin' him out, though. I don't wear no guns to do my job in here. Mostly jest some rowdy miners, you know, that kinda stuff."

"His name?" I reminded Sarge.

"Goes by Preacher," he said. "Preacher Dalton. I don't think he knows much about the good book, though."

I could tell Sarge was getting mighty uncomfortable with this, so I changed the subject while I finished off the beer. Sarge stuck to his one, plus maybe a half.

I stopped off to talk with Holt for a while about the bar. He said things were good, but there *were more rowdies around lately*, and asked me to check in at the Suds 'n Such a little more often. I noticed he glanced down at my Colt when he said it.

I promised Holt I would do that and glanced around the room one time before I left. Everything seemed pretty normal. Sarge gave me a nod as I left. I was going to walk down to Joanna's Bakery, but first, I decided to go the other way for a few steps to look for this land agent Sarge had talked about.

That didn't take long. I saw a sign that read *Land Agent* just a couple doors over from the Suds 'n Such. I didn't see a name out front anywhere. I glanced in the window on the way by. There was a guy, maybe my age and height, narrow shoulders, talking to the mayor. He gave me a sharp-eyed look as I went past. I crossed the street and started back toward the bakery, thinking over the things Sarge had just told me.

I rode south out of Silverton two days later. I didn't have a real good idea of where to find ranch land, but the elevation was a little lower south of town. That might give me a just a little longer growing season. That sounded good to me. I had spent some time yesterday looking north of town, but I hadn't seen any vacant land that looked good to me. I'd stopped to talk to guys working in the fields a time or two, but they didn't seem to have any tips on ranches for sale.

The railroad tracks from Durango led me out of town to the south. I decided to go east from the tracks a bit to look for land. Where I saw pastures I could use for grazing and hay crops, the mountains lifted to the skies just beyond the pastures, with pine, aspen, and spruce trees covering the hillsides as they rose. Wild-flowers dotted the fields.

After an hour of searching, I saw something that

caught my attention. I saw people loading up two wagons outside a farmhouse. Smoke lifted from a chimney in the house. The land stretched out to the mountains beyond, and I thought I could see a river cutting through the pasture. I had an idea there were elk out there in the hills and meadows. I sat and watched for a while. I could see maybe a few cattle. It looked like they were leaving a half-grown hay crop behind.

After a couple minutes of watching, I touched my heels to my horse and rode up to have a talk with them. I could see and man and a teen-aged boy doing the heavy lifting, putting a piece or two of furniture up on one wagon. A woman and a young girl were putting some boxes on the other wagon.

Behind them, I could see a big man sitting on the porch. He had some broad shoulders, a bald head shaped like a bullet, and had *muscles on his muscles*, as my ma would have said. He didn't seem to lift a hand to help with the moving.

I pushed my hat back on my head. "Moving out?" I asked.

The man turned to look at me. I noticed he glanced sideways at Bullet-Head on the porch before he answered. "Yep," he said. "Moving on."

I glanced over at Bullet-Head, who was glaring at me and sizing up the Colt on my hip.

"Is this land for sale?" I asked in a low tone.

The man shot another glance over at the porch. "Got the land listed with a land agent in town," he said, loud enough for Bullet-Head to hear easily. "He'll take care of it for me. We're headed back to Missouri."

"Okay," I said loudly, then moved to turn my horse back to the trail. "What if a private buyer offered you a better price?" I muttered over my shoulder. "Would you be interested in that?"

He turned his back to the porch and pretended to push a box farther back in the wagon. "Could be, mister," he said softly. "I kin talk to you at the bakery in town, two days from now, in the mawnin'. If'n yore interested, I would have to have some cash and move mighty fast." He turned back toward the house. I saw Bullet-Head relax back on the steps.

"See ya," I hollered and rode back to the trail.

"Well now," I mumbled to myself as I rode back toward town. Somebody was making sure these folks moved off the property. The man must not be getting a good price from the land agent, which was no surprise to me after what Sarge had said.

The man was taking a chance, meeting me at the bakery. That had to be Joanna's place. It was the only bakery in Silverton. I would bring enough cash to close the deal if he was serious. I had to hope he would bring whatever papers he had for this property. That was if the land agent didn't have them already, I realized.

One other thought struck me as I reached town. This rancher might need some help to get himself and his family out of town if he sold to me. I might have to help them load up on the train or guard the family and wagons for a while on the trail out of town if he wasn't taking the train.

Who, I wondered to myself as I prepared to go into the Suds 'n Such, was Bullet-Head, the thug sitting on the porch? Hired muscle, no doubt about that. Someone had probably forced the man and his family off the land. But who was Bullet-Head working for? That was the question.

I could sense trouble just as soon as I stepped into the saloon. It was way too quiet, that's the first thing I noticed. I stepped in a little farther and I could see somebody was covering Holt with a drawn pistol. Holt had both his hands on the bar, but I knew there was a shotgun under the bar right where he was standing. I had never seen the man with the drawn pistol.

Looking over a little farther, I saw a tall man in a battered black hat with his back to me. His hand hovered near his right-hand gun. He was facing Sarge, who stood facing both of us. I knew Sarge was unarmed.

I took a step closer, and the guy with the drawn gun at the bar flicked a sideways glance at me. He took a look at the Colt on my hip, then spoke over his shoulder.

"Preacher!" was all he said.

The guy in the suspenders turned slowly toward me, finally turning to face me directly.

"Preacher," I said. I remembered what Sarge had said about him. "I guess you know a lot about the good book?"

He stared at me, not bothering to answer. The guy covering Holt started to turn in my direction, then swung back quickly when He saw Holt's hand move.

"There's two of us," Preacher said, leaning over to spit tobacco on the floor. "Just one of you."

I never took my eyes off him as I answered. "Holt," I said. "That shotgun has two barrels, don't it?"

"Yup," he answered. Holt could talk your leg off all day, but just didn't seem to have many words when he was ready for a scrap.

"Hard to miss with two barrels up close," I said to the guy named Preacher. "Plus, there's a lot of folks behind you that probably don't like you much. Might be hard to get outta here with your hide in one piece."

His eyes slid down to my Colt, then back up. "You've got a gun," he said. "Maybe this could just be about you and me."

"It could," I agreed, "but I'm gonna promise you won't leave here on your own two feet. Now, that buddy of yours might get some lead into me, but his own mama won't recognize him after he soaks up two barrels of that shotgun. Or else Holt could give you a barrel apiece if I don't manage to quite finish you off. Then, I'm thinkin' you'll have quite a problem gettin' out of town, what with all the folks that've seen this."

I could see some surprise in his eyes. He was used to men backing down from him. He likely had a bit of a name as a gunfighter. I hadn't backed down, and I'd put in his head that he probably couldn't escape without taking a bullet or a piece of a shotgun blast.

I thought he might also be wondering what I meant about getting out of town. Truth is, I just threw that out there as a shot in the dark. I had no idea if this town would back me up. Nobody wants a mob rounding him up and swinging him from the nearest tree, though. That was something else to worry about.

It seemed like we were all just frozen there for several minutes. Probably, it was just a few seconds, but those were some mighty long seconds. I could still see this Preacher guy, with Sarge behind him, and the other gunman trying to watch both me and Holt.

Me, I wanted to make sure I remembered this Preacher guy. He looked a tad taller than my six foot one, and several pounds heavier than my one-ninety. Had a big hook nose on him. Mostly, though, I watched those eyes. If they're gonna go for their gun, you can see it in the eyes first.

THREE
A WARNING

The thing that had me worried the most was wondering if that guy covering Holt might just shoot him point-blank and wheel around on me. He had to know he would be hunted down and hung for murder if he did that. No question at all. It wasn't a fair shooting if he just pulled the trigger now. That didn't mean he was thinkin' this stuff out, though.

I kept my concentration on Preacher's eyes. I could almost see the ciphering he was doing in that noggin of his right now. First, he would have to put me down without soaking up any bullets while he did it. Then he had to worry about what would happen over there at the bar. If he wound up looking down the barrel of a shotgun, his chances weren't good.

He blinked for the first time, then blinked again. I took that as a good sign. His eyes wandered over toward the bar, then his hand came away from his gun belt. He spoke in a low growl.

"Bert." That was aimed at the guy covering Holt.

The gravelly tone took me by surprise. I could see there were scars across his neck. I wondered if he'd escaped a hanging noose somewhere back down the road. Maybe that's what gave him that gravelly voice.

Bert, over at the bar, eased his gun back into the holster and stepped away. They stood side-by-side and backed out of the saloon. You could almost hear the sighs of relief when they walked away.

Holt pulled the shotgun from under the bar and took a look around the room, almost challenging anybody else to make trouble. The troublemakers were gone, though. Everybody went back to drinking and playing cards.

Sarge walked across the room to me. "'Preciate ya," he said simply. "He wanted to gun me down after I caught him cheatin' at poker. He saw I didn't have a gun and then he didn't know what to do. Holt's gonna have to keep that shotgun a little handier if those boys come back."

I gave Sarge a pat on the shoulder, waved at Holt, and left the saloon. Now I had met Preacher. Sort of. I doubted either of us would forget the other. He struck me as a pretty salty customer. He wasn't scared of me or panicky. He'd just figgered his odds, cool as could be, and decided he didn't like 'em. That didn't mean he might not like them better next time. I'd best keep that in mind.

I sat in the café, watching my old friend and boss, Cleo Ward, and wondering why he'd come up here to see me. More than that, I'd run into him on my way to Joanna's Bakery, and he'd insisted on talking to me here, not at the bakery. I had a feeling he didn't want Joanna to worry about the things he'd come to tell me. It turned out I was right about that.

He stirred a spoon around in his coffee and got to the point, just like he always did. He leaned forward. "You ever hear of The Royal Gorge War?" he asked me.

I scrunched up my forehead and thought about it. "I know a little bit," I told him. "It was about two railroads fightin' over who would get to build a line through that gorge, right? Over near Canon City, over east of here."

Ward looked just a bit surprised. "Right," he agreed. "It was mostly over by the time you got here from Texas that this stuff happened."

It looked like Ward was getting ready to tell a long story. I waved around to get a cup of coffee for myself and settled in.

"It started when they found silver up there in Leadville," he said. He pointed out the window. I'm thinkin' he was pointing north. I knew that's where Leadville was.

"There were two railroads that right away wanted to build a rail line to Leadville on account of that silver. One was my railroad, and the one you worked for, the Denver and Rio Grande. The other was the Atchison, Topeka, and Santa Fe. We always just call it the Santa Fe."

I nodded. The Santa Fe was a bigger railroad, I

knew, and already had some connections down south to Arizona.

"We were closer. We had tracks built to just a couple miles east of Canon City. The line had to go from Canon City to Leadville, which meant it had to go through some mighty nasty country called The Royal Gorge. Santa Fe got the jump on us and started building rails through the gorge. We took 'em to court."

Ward shook his head. "It got ugly real fast. While things were going around and around in court, they were laying rails. We built a fort at both ends and tried to discourage those boys."

"Discourage 'em how?" I asked.

Ward made a face. "Rolled rocks down at 'em, things like that. Maybe fired a few shots. I wasn't there." He shook his head again and took a sip of his coffee. "Guns got hired after that. More by Santa Fe than by us. They had Bat Masterson and Doc Holliday up there at one point. They took over the forts."

This was news to me. He got my attention when he said Masterson and Holliday were in on this. Ward kept going. "We won in court. Denver and Rio Grande, I mean. We got the rights to build that line, but we couldn't keep Masterson and his boy out of those forts. Finally, D&RG got up some troops they hired and stormed the forts. Drove 'em out the back door and took over."

Ward leaned back. "Anyway," he said. "Let's keep the story short."

If this was a short story, I didn't want to hear the

long one. I looked around and waved to get myself another cup of coffee.

"We made a truce and settled it down, finally," Ward said. "My railroad, the D&RG, got the rights, and we're running the line through Royal Gorge. Masterson and most of his boys moved on after a while."

He squinted across the table at me. "There were some bad hombres that got into this war, and not all of 'em moved on. That's what I came to talk to you about."

I hunched down in my seat a little. I didn't like where this was going. I could start to see why he didn't want to talk about it in Joanna's Bakery.

"I came to tell you about a couple of these guys that I've heard are operating right here around Silverton," he said. "Names I think ought to keep your ears perked up about. One was a guy who worked in the offices of the Santa Fe. Fancies himself a tough guy, too, but mostly he gets others to follow his orders. Goes by the name of Ike Penfield."

He stopped and looked to see if I knew that name. I shook my head.

Ward nodded. "He's the kind of guy you might not see or hear of until he sticks a knife in your back. Keep your ears up for that name. I heard he's buying up land, robbing miners, stealing cattle, whatever can make him some good money." He paused. "I know you want to buy some land, right?"

I nodded.

"That's why I think you might run into him," Ward said. "And maybe even in town. He might have his hand in around here, too, paying off sheriffs or forcing shops and businesses to pay him money."

I thought about Joanna's Bakery and the Suds 'n Such saloon and winced a little. Holt and I could take care of ourselves. Would they be low enough to go after a bakery or the girl who owned it?

Ward waited, watching my face. "The other'n is a gunfighter. Pretty salty, too, from what I hear. Had a run-in or two with Masterson and Holliday, then left that crew before the end of the war. Came back when those guys left and set up his own little crew. I'm not for sure he's tied in with Penfield, but I wouldn't be surprised."

I had a feeling I knew what name I was about to hear. I just waited.

"Preacher Dalton is this guy's name. You ever hear of him or run into him?"

I told him the story about what had just happened at the saloon. Ward gave a low whistle and looked out the window. "Those boys still here in town, or did they ride off?"

"Rode off, I think," I told him.

Ward traced a pattern on the table with his finger. "Well," he said, "he won't bushwhack you, from what I hear. He'll give you a fair, stand-up fight, but he's sure enough gonna want a fight with you after this morning. You'd best step careful. He'll always try to give himself an edge."

We stood and dropped a coin or two on the table for the coffee. We went out and I walked Ward back down to the railroad station. Now I knew why he'd made this special trip to talk to me. Sometimes, a man's life can depend on knowin' the things he needs to know. This was for sure something I'd needed to know about.

I thanked Ward and saw him off on the train back to Durango. Somewhere on the way to Joanna's Bakery, I just took a seat on a bench, pushed my hat back, and did some thinkin' about what Ward had just told me. It didn't make any difference about going ahead with my plans. Once I make up my mind to do something, I'm pretty much gonna see it through. I would just have to be careful.

━━━

Joanna had put a bell on the door at the bakery. That took me by surprise for just a second, but I soon forgot about it when she came over to give me a kiss at the door and show me to a table. I waited while she said goodbye to a couple other customers, then we had the place to ourselves.

She seated herself next to me at the table and looked at me. "What is it?" she asked. "What's going on?"

Well, I thought, so much for keeping the bad news to myself. She had sniffed this one out right from the start. I decided to tell her everything except the part about Penfield and Preacher Dalton maybe being connected and trying to strong-arm the whole town. I wasn't even sure about that part myself, so no use in getting her worried about that until I knew more.

I told her the rest of the stuff Ward had come to tell me and proceeded to explain about the standoff at the

Suds 'n Such this morning. I finished by telling her about my visit to the ranch south of town and how the owner would meet me right here in the morning. I told her I was hoping to buy the property.

She blinked a few times. That was a lot to soak up in one sitting, but I knew she could handle it. She'd been through some tough times, just like me. She seemed to be sorting through things in her head, trying to decide which question to ask me first.

"This guy Preacher, did you say he's left town? What does he look like, anyway? I might have seen him."

"He's gone for now," I answered, "but that doesn't mean he's gone for good. I don't think he was just passing through." I went on to describe him, as best I good. That black hat had been down kinda low on his forehead, so I was a little short on details.

Joanna looked thoughtful. "I don't think he's been in here, and I haven't seen him around town, for what that's worth. I'll let you know if I do." She moved on with her next question.

"What are you going to do about buying that land? Do you still want it if somebody has their goon watching the place? I guess they're doing that because somebody's trying to just about steal the property?" She sat back and watched me with a knowing look in her eye.

"When have you ever known me to back down from a fight?" I demanded.

She shook her head, then started to smile, then finally chuckled. "That would be never," she agreed. "I guess that's part of why I love you." She shook a finger at me. "You'd better be careful, Latigo Smith," she warned.

Well, she was right about that. I hadn't drawn a real good hand so far in Silverton. That wasn't new for me, but I might be up against a lot of tough hombres around here. I promised to be careful.

"Tomorrow morning, though," I said, "I'm going to come with enough cash to make a good, fair offer for that property. I'm going to have $3,000 with me. If he takes it, I might have to help him move in a hurry to get his family and things on the first train out of town."

She didn't bat an eye. "What can I do?"

I thought about it. "Be prepared to close the bakery for a little while and maybe help get the wife and kids on the train along with their things. Movin' fast is gonna be the key. If they can get away far enough and fast enough, it won't be worth anybody's time to chase them down."

"Done," she said. She went off to get my usual breakfast, then sat down and chatted with me, getting up only every once in a while to see to a new customer. As always, I felt more peaceful with her around.

I was at least feeling better about things since she'd said she hadn't seen Preacher around here. Maybe Penfield and Preacher and whoever else was in on this would leave her alone.

When I left, I strolled down to the train station to find out what time in the morning the train left. I might need to get that family aboard right when the whistle blew. Then I headed for the land agent's office.

I was curious if he would offer me the property I'd looked at yesterday.

I took an extra look at the sign and the window when I walked into the land agent's office. His name wasn't showing anywhere, but I knew this must be Aaron Budge. I walked in and took a seat across from where he sat with his dirty boots propped up on the edge of his desk. He gave me a long, sharp-eyed look.

Finally, he took a long drag from a nasty-smelling cigar and a big slurp from his coffee. At least, I thought it was coffee. Who knows? He thumped his boots down on the floor and mumbled something that sounded like "Help you?"

This, I thought, is somebody that don't need to make any money to the likes of me, somebody just walking in off the street. His money was comin' from somewhere else, and it had the smell of dirty money to me.

"I'm lookin' to buy a ranch around here for some high grazing and maybe raise some hay," I told him. "I can probly pay cash money, maybe depending on what the prices are around here. I'm new in town," I added.

"Hmmph." He took another long drag and another slurp and looked at me like this didn't interest him a bit, not even the part about cash. "Whereabouts around town you thinkin'? North, south, whaddya want?"

"South of town, I'm thinking. Maybe close to two

hundred acres, something like that. Not quite as high on that side as north of town, maybe get a little longer growing season."

I knew I'd described the land I'd been looking at yesterday pretty well, but not enough to let him know I was on to something. I shut up and waited to hear what he had to say.

He was already shaking his head, but he yanked open a desk drawer and plopped a bunch of papers on the desk. He went through them, stopping to look every once in a while, then shaking his head. He was puttin' on a pretty good show for me, I thought.

"Nuthin' like that," he announced, shoving the papers back into the drawer. He took another slurp from the cup and stared at the ceiling. "Got somethin' just west, kinda on the edge of town. Mebbe twenty, twenty-five acres. You could start with that."

"Fenced?" I asked. "Anything to keep the cows from wandering into town?"

"Nah," he said, shaking his head again. "You could grow some hay, though. Get it right to market on the railroad here in town."

"Not interested," I said flatly. "Nothing south of town, maybe up against the mountains, to help keep the cows from wandering off?"

"Got nuthin' like that. Had somethin' last week, but it's done been sold." Those eyes looked a little suspicious for the first time. Time for me to go, I decided. "Thanks anyway," I said, closing the door softly behind me. I had the feeling his eyes were watching me as I headed back to Holt's saloon. I was hoping I hadn't tipped my hand on this one.

I stepped inside and looked around for Sarge. Holt pointed at the storage room in the back. "He's tidyin' up back there," Holt explained. "Sometimes he takes a nap back there when it's slow. Dunno which he's doing right now."

I found Sarge moving some boxes around. "Got a minute?" I asked.

"Sure. Beats hauling these boxes around. They don't get no lighter the older I get." He followed me out to a table.

"Got a little time in the morning, maybe around nine or ten o'clock?" I asked. "There's free breakfast for you in the deal."

He brightened up and nodded. "That's before this place opens up, anyway. Is the breakfast at Joanna's Bakery?"

"It is," I told him. "I might need you to keep a couple varmints off my back while I get a family out of town." I went on and explained what was happening.

FOUR
RANCH FOR SALE

I kept tipping my chair back at my table by the bakery window and looking out at the street that morning, wondering if my guy was going to come, what time he would come, and would he have his family with him?

I had my $3,000 stashed in a cupboard back there in Joanna's kitchen. Sarge, who had taken to wearing a gun belt and a Colt, was loafing on a bench across the street from the bakery. I didn't see any sign of Bullet-Head, who'd been taking up space on the porch when I'd paid a visit to the ranch I wanted to buy.

I checked the clock standing in the corner. It was only 7:30 in the morning. Joanna had been open for a half hour. She had customers at two of the tables and a line of three miners getting coffee and pastries. I waited for her to finish with her customers before following her back into the kitchen.

"Do you have room for me to set up a small table back here in the kitchen?" I blurted.

She swung around to look at me, confusion written on her face. "Whatever for?" she asked.

"If the rancher"—I realized suddenly I didn't even know his name—"brings his wife and kids and hopes to make a quick trip out of town, I'd like to have them out of sight back here. If the people trying to control the land sales see the family, it'll tip 'em off. I'd like to get the family out of here quietly, like maybe out the back. Down to the train station, or whatever he wants to do."

Joanna nodded quickly and helped me drag a small table and three chairs back into the corner of the kitchen. I moved back to the dining area out front and peered out the window. Sarge was still in place across the street. While I watched, a buggy pulled up in front of the bakery. It was the rancher with his family and a few bags in the back of the buggy.

I darted out the front and motioned for him to follow down the side alley. We parked the buggy in the back of the bakery. I knew we were already too late, though. I had seen a big man with a bald head on a big buckskin horse trailing the wagon down the street.

We left the wagon in the back. Maybe we could confuse Bullet-Head a bit about where the wife and family had gone. The wife and kids followed me inside and took a seat at the table in the kitchen. Joanna moved to bring pastries for the family, coffee for the mom, and juice for the kids.

"What's your name?" I mumbled to the rancher as we moved back to a table in the front room. Bullet-Head had dismounted outside and was moving toward the front door. Across the street, I could see the guy who had been in the Suds 'n Such with Preacher Dalton yesterday.

Not good, I thought to myself, they've brought a gunman and a brawler to stop this. I watched as Sarge positioned himself at the corner of the building across the street. From there, he could move up behind the gunman without being seen. I would have to count on Sarge to keep that guy out of the fight.

We sat down at a table and the rancher answered my question. "Jed," he told me. "Jed Swann." He looked at the front door anxiously as Bullet-Head came in and moved to the counter to get some coffee.

"What about Otis?" Jed hissed.

"Otis?"

He inclined his head at the thug I'd been calling Bullet-Head

"Don't worry about him," I murmured. "I'll keep him off you. And the gunman across the street. I've got him covered, too." I glanced around as Otis took a seat across the room. "Do you want to get out of town right away if we agree on a price? I've got cash here with me," I added.

"Yup," Jed said, barely moving his lips. "We want to catch a train straight out of here. We want to go back to her folks' place in Missouri for a while. What can you offer? I've got one hundred eighty acres of good grazing land and good water. Stream cuts across the middle of my pasture."

"Three thousand, cash money," I said. "I've got the money stashed in a cupboard back there in the kitchen."

"I'll take it," he blurted. "It's twice what Penfield and his thugs offered me. I've got a signed title to the land in my pocket."

We paused while Joanna came to serve us coffee. I shielded my face with one hand while I spoke to her. "In a minute," I said, "Jed, here, is gonna come back there to the kitchen. Give him the money I have in the cupboard. He has a title to his land in his pocket. Keep it for me when he gives it to you. Let them out the back door."

She nodded and moved away. We stayed at the table for a few minutes, sipping coffee. I was hoping Otis would finish his coffee and move outside to wait, but he didn't look like he was going anywhere.

After five minutes had passed, I knew I had to get this family moving before more thugs showed up. So far, it was even. If any more came, we would be outgunned.

"Time to go," I said. "Just head for the kitchen back there, get the money from Joanna, give her the title, and get out to the buggy. Train leaves in about a half hour. I'll keep 'em off your back until then."

He nodded, stood, and moved toward the back. Otis watched him go, trying to make up his mind. When Jed didn't come out of the kitchen after a minute passed, he stood and moved that way. Behind me, I could hear the back door close.

I moved to block his way. "That's just the kitchen," I said. "Just for the folks who work here at the bakery."

He reached out to push me out of the way. I grabbed his hand and twisted his arm behind his back, shoving him up against the wall. He let out a roar and tried to stomp down on my ankle with his boot.

Joanna hustled out from the back, cocking a Colt 1849 pocket revolver. I stared. I didn't know she had it. She laid it up against Otis's ribs.

"Take it outside," she snarled. "If you bust this place up, I'll give you a taste of this Colt. Outside!"

He nodded and relaxed, leaning with his head against the wall. I let go of his wrist and stood back. He moved around me and toward the front door. I followed him. We could have this fight sooner or we could have it later. It might as well be sooner.

As we came out the door, the gunman across the street straightened up and moved toward us, his hand dropping toward his gun belt. I saw Sarge appear from the alley between the buildings. He pulled his gun, reversed it, and brought the man down with a blow to his head.

Otis swung suddenly and charged me, reaching up to wrap me up and take me down. I sidestepped. He reached out as he went past, trying to circle my waist with his arm and take me down. I brought my elbow down hard, right above his kidneys. He let out a gasp and went to his knees.

I stepped out to the street to take the fight a little farther away from the bakery. I could see Sarge hauling the unconscious gunman into the alleyway. He turned and trotted toward me, his gun still out.

"Train station!" I shouted. "Get them on that train and out of town. I'll take care of this guy." Sarge turned and trotted down the street.

Otis came slowly off his knees and moved to the

street, circling me slowly, looking a little wary this time. I circled with him, watching. I knew now he was a grappler, not a puncher. He wanted to take me down and put his boots to me. I couldn't let him get me off my feet.

He charged me again, then stopped and swung a wild right at my head. I sidestepped it easily and swung a hard right to the side of his head. He stopped in his tracks and shook his head like an angry bear. Probably trying to stop the ringing, I thought.

He charged again, moving so suddenly it caught me by surprise. I backpedaled, off balance, then fell over backward, bringing my knees up to my chest. He landed on top of me, clawing at my eyes. I straightened my legs and shoved him off me, letting his momentum carry him over the top. He landed heavily behind me in the street.

I rolled to my feet, but he'd come up a lot faster than I'd expected. He didn't quite get his feet under him and came in low. I swung a straight right and split his lip open. He sagged against me, still trying to wrap me up, so I lifted a knee into his rib cage. He went to his knees heavily.

I circled him slowly. He was finished, but I wasn't sure he knew it. I stood back and waited.

He came off the ground one more time, grabbing his ribs and moaning, then lurched toward me again. I lifted a left uppercut to the point of his jaw and he fell forward on his face, out cold.

I grabbed him by the shoulders and hauled him across the street and into the alleyway next to the guy Sarge had knocked out. Then I let go of him and bent over with my hands on my knees, sucking down some air. That guy had to be about two-fifty if he was #on ounce, I thought. That was a lot of dead weight.

The gunman stirred and moaned, so I trotted back across the street to get two lengths of rope from my saddlebag. I came back and rolled the gunman onto his belly, then tied his hands behind his back.

Otis was already face down the way I'd left him and still not moving, so I tied his hands too, then trotted down toward the train station, hoping things were more peaceful down there.

They had boarded the train by the time I got there. I could see Jed and his wife through the window of a car up front near the engine. Sarge was standing by the door to the car, arms crossed, studying the passengers as they boarded.

I trotted up to the car and waved at Jed and his wife when they saw me. She mouthed the words *thank you*, and I nodded. In another minute, the whistle blew and they moved away, headed back to some familiar ground in Missouri.

I took a minute to check myself over and see if I had any injuries I didn't know about. There was a sore spot along my right rib cage, and my lips seemed to be puffy, so I must have soaked up a few blows I didn't remember. Still, against a huge guy like Otis, I counted myself pretty lucky.

Sarge watched while I explored my injuries, then moved back toward the station. "What's next, slugger?" he asked.

I stared back up the street toward the bakery.

"Well," I grumbled. "I didn't even get to finish my coffee. You want some?"

Sarge fell into step beside me as we went back to the bakery for some coffee and breakfast. I watched the train disappear around a corner up ahead, then it hit me. I was now the owner of a ranch.

I settled back down at my usual table in the bakery while Joanna joined us with breakfast for us both. When she gave me a hug, I was pretty sure she was still carrying the Colt 1849 under her apron. I grinned a little. This was a frontier girl.

"I saw you tie those guys up across the street," she reminded me. "How long do you plan to leave them over there?"

I had completely forgotten them. I went out, pulled a knife from my saddlebag, and continued across the street. I found them where I'd left them. Both were conscious now, and from the way they greeted me, I could tell I wasn't their favorite.

I pulled the gun from the belt of the guy Sarge had knocked out, emptied the bullets and put them in my pocket, then returned the gun to his belt. I checked Otis for weapons and found none. He'd been counting on using his fists and getting me down on the ground, I guess.

I cut them both loose and stood back. Neither of them seemed like they were ready to tangle with me again, but Otis sent a glare in my direction as he mounted up.

"This ain't over," he snarled.

I just nodded. "I'm pretty sure you know where to find me," I told him. "You and whoever it is you're working for."

I rejoined Joanna and Sarge in the bakery. Joanna gave me a questioning look while I tucked into my eggs and coffee.

I just shrugged. "Who wants to see my new ranch?" I asked.

Ike Penfield stared out the back windows of his office in Leadville, Colorado. He thought of it as his office, even though it had been built as a dance hall. The windows and front door were all boarded up. Having the entire building to himself suited Penfield just fine. He had a bed in one corner at the back and a desk in the opposite corner. Nobody bothered him here.

Ike could hear horses and wagons going by on the main street out front and sometimes shouts and the occasional gunshot. He grinned a little to himself. This was his kind of place for at least as long as it lasted. Wide open boomtown with no rules. No rules that got enforced, anyway.

He could see the hillsides out the back window. They were covered with fresh diggings. Not everybody that was digging out there was hitting pay dirt, but folks knew Leadville as the Silver City for good reason. Miners, outlaws, people looking for a handout, business people, you name it—they had all come to Leadville. That gave Ike Penfield and his men a lot of targets. Fools waiting to be separated from their money.

Penfield had lost track of how many people he had working for him. Most of them worked the trails in and out of Leadville, robbing miners and sometimes settlers moving in with valuables. He owned three of the six saloons in town and both of the gambling halls.

Not bad, Penfield thought, considering he'd had to find a whole new way to make money after the railroad war had settled down. He scowled as he stared out the window, remembering how that had turned out.

Ike Penfield had come to Colorado to make money off the war over Royal Gorge. He had hired out to the Atchison, Topeka, and Santa Fe railroad, and then hired a few guns to help him get the job done. Then Bat Masterson and Doc Holliday had come and made it clear they were going to run the crews.

Penfield prided himself on his gun skills and might have considered taking on Masterson. It was Holliday he was scared of. The man was crazy. Like he didn't care if he lived or died, that's how Holliday was. Penfield wanted to live.

He'd cleared out after that. The one good thing about that railroad war was that he'd met Preacher Dalton. Preacher didn't mind using his guns, and Penfield found lots of work for him and those guns of his. Preacher kept people in line, kept money flowing along to Penfield. That way, Penfield could keep getting richer and keep his hands clean.

The biggest problem he had now was moving the stolen ore out of town for sale. He'd accumulated a lot of businesses, and now he'd seen how valuable land could be. He was building up a lot of that, too, but Penfield was a careful man. He'd been to prison once, and that was enough for a lifetime. In a few years, the saloons and gambling houses in Leadville would be gone. Penfield knew that. He would own ranches and banks by then. Maybe he would even be a senator or the governor of Colorado.

Movement outside the window caught his eye. He watched as Preacher stepped out from the path through the woods that led to his back door. He'd had to trust somebody to keep things running while he built up his legal holdings and made his plans for his future. Preacher was the guy he'd trusted.

Penfield felt a moment of fear while he watched Preacher approach the back door. Maybe, he thought, he'd trusted Preacher too much. Maybe the man knew more than he should. What would he do if Preacher went against him?

Penfield soothed his fears and moved to open the back door. He'd had to trust somebody, hadn't he? He could take down Preacher if he had to. Meanwhile, he needed an update on how things were going down in Silverton.

Silverton was the newest boomtown. Penfield was acquiring land down there for reasons he'd shared with nobody. The Denver and Rio Grande Railroad had built a line through to Durango, and they were moving a lot of ore out of Silverton.

Silverton was going to be Penfield's next stop, and hopefully his last. Leadville was big—it was the second largest city in Colorado now. Only Denver was bigger. Leadville would die down, though. Boom-towns always did. The money he'd made in Leadville was dirty money. Money that could send him back to prison.

In Silverton, he would be a respected landowner and business owner. He'd start with just one saloon. Then maybe a bank to go with all the property he was accumulating down there. His money had already gotten the mayor elected, even if that fool didn't know it. Penfield would pull all the strings in Silverton. Maybe he would let Preacher take over what was left up here. The more he thought about that, the better he liked it. He would sever all ties with Preacher.

He opened the door and let Preacher into his office. Preacher took a seat opposite the desk and Penfield settled himself on the other side. He was looking to get himself a saloon and maybe a bank in Silverton, and he was building some land holdings outside the town. He needed to hear how that was going.

Penfield folded his hand across his lap and waited for Preacher's report.

FIVE
KING OF SILVERTON

It started with the twitch at the corner of the left eye. Preacher Dalton had noticed that before. When Penfield didn't like something he was hearing, there was a twitch at the corner of the eye. After that came a flush that started at the base of the neck and worked its way up. That was happening now, too. No matter, Preacher had to get through this report and wait out the explosion that came next. He'd been through this before.

Preacher had finished the part about how he and Bert got backed down in the Suds 'n Such Saloon. He knew Penfield had already decided he would be the one who owned that saloon, so this was definitely bad news. He'd given Preacher orders to drive out the current owner, Holt. Preacher watched while the flush climbed a little higher up Penfield's neck.

"Who backed you idiots down in that saloon?" Penfield snarled.

Preacher ignored that part about being an idiot. He

reminded himself how good the pay had been. He shrugged. "Some drifter, old-time army guy that calls himself Sarge," he muttered. "We was ready for him an' the owner, that guy named Holt. Some other guy come in, taken us by surprise."

Penfield watched, the tic at the corner of the left eye getting worse. "Who?" he barked. "This guy got a name?"

"I asked around," Preacher answered, meeting the stare he was getting from Penfield. "Goes by the name of Latigo Smith. Used to work for the D&RG railroad, that's what they say. Got some sand," he admitted grudgingly.

Penfield just watched him, the way a hawk watches a mouse, Preacher thought. One of these days, Penfield might have to find out who was the mouse and who was the hawk. Good money could only keep Preacher quiet for just so long.

"There's more," he blurted. "Has to do with that ranch you wanted to buy. The one Budge made an offer on. That property that's got the railroad tracks at the far end."

Now Penfield got quiet. This was new. Preacher shifted a little in his chair so he could reach his Colt a little faster if he needed to. Quiet meant dangerous with a guy like this. Preacher had seen this kind of thing before.

"Sodbuster what owned that ranch got out of town. Looks like this Latigo Smith guy bought the property. I had Bert and Otis watching the sodbuster. They got theirselves busted up some, Bert and Otis did. Sodbuster, his wife, an' their chillun hauled it all outta town."

"Was it Smith?" The entire face had gone red now, but the voice was quiet. Preacher watched Penfield's hands—they were both on top of the desk and they weren't moving. That was good. At least for now.

"Yup. Latigo Smith taken Otis down, knuckle and skull. That Sarge guy snuck up on Bert and slugged him upside his head. Got him a goose egg on the side of his noggin, Bert does. Otis is missin' a couple teeth, got some busted ribs, and a split lip. I taken both of 'em down to the doc to get fixed up."

Seconds passed while they exchanged glares. Finally, Penfield swung and stared out the window. Preacher inched his hand closer to his Colt and watched Penfield's hands, now on the arms of his chair. When he swung back from the window, Penfield kept his hands in view and placed them back on the desk carefully. He still needed Preacher, he reminded himself. He reached for a glass of water on his desk and sipped it slowly while he calmed himself.

"What about that worthless nephew of mine, Knowles?" he said slowly, emphasizing the name. "I made him the mayor down there. What's he doing about this? Did he get a sheriff yet?"

Preacher nodded slowly. "He got him a sheriff just the other day. Pretty green kid, if you're askin' me. Done about a year in the army, but he ain't seen no real fightin', that's what I heard. Name is Moore."

Penfield stared at his hands. "You tell my nephew," he hissed, "to run Latigo Smith out of town. Send Otis and

Bert and whoever else they need back in to bust up that saloon. Bust up that Sarge guy while they're at it. If Bert and Otis fail again, maybe you need to take care of that. Make that sheriff earn his pay, too, or I'll get a new one."

Preacher Dalton waited several seconds until he realized Penfield had finished talking. Preacher nodded, rose slowly, and angled toward the door, never turning his back on Penfield. This was a whole new side of the man, a more dangerous side. At the door, he stopped and turned around.

"I'll need a couple guys," he said.

Penfield stared, then nodded. "You need a gunhand or muscle?"

Preacher considered that one. "One of each," he said. "Tell 'em to meet me at the café in Silverton." He left without waiting for an answer.

Preacher eased out of the door and stood outside for a minute. He reached into his pocket, pulled out a cigar, and lit it. He moved sideways off the porch and around the building. He would find his way back to his horse without exposing himself to gunfire from Penfield's window. He would make the easy money for a while longer. He'd be watching Penfield, though. The guy was mean as a snake, he could feel it.

Penfield swung around to watch as Preacher Dalton left. He would hold off on that move down to Silverton until things were under control a little better. He could wait for a while. No need to expose himself just yet. Once this Latigo Smith had been taken out of the picture, he could make his move.

Penfield watched from the corner of his eye as Preacher disappeared from sight around the corner of the building. Preacher got things done, that's why Penfield used him. At least until now, he got things done. Preacher, he knew, had some kind of idea about fair fights and straight-up shootouts. "Have to give a man his chance," he always said.

Penfield got up to find his whiskey bottle. If Preacher could get things done his way, that was good. Penfield had to give him that chance. Much cleaner that way. Maybe Preacher could get rid of this Latigo Smith and get him that saloon and that ranch property doing it his way. Penfield had gotten himself several hundred acres near the railroad already, but he needed the one Smith had taken. That one had the best access to the railroad line. If Preacher couldn't get it done his way, Penfield would do it himself.

He downed half the whiskey and set the glass carefully on the desk. Straight-up fights were a sucker's game. Penfield got up and let himself out the back door. Maybe he would go down to one of his gaming halls tonight and watch while the suckers gave him their money. He would be the king of Silverton soon enough.

━━━

I spread out a blanket on the grass behind the farmhouse while Joanna spread out the lunch she had brought for us. The chicken and potato salad looked delicious. I got my hand slapped when I reached for the cookies.

Joanna wagged a finger at me. "After you've had your lunch, Latigo Smith."

I massaged my hand, grinned, and watched as Sarge rode up to join us. "Mighty good grazing land," he said. "Got yerself a good stream runnin' through. There's still a few head grazing out there. I expect they're yours now. He probly couldn't get 'em all rounded up and sold on short notice."

About an hour later, Sarge was sprawled on his back, making little snoring noises. I had stuffed myself with Joanna's lunch, but managed to stay upright while we leaned against a log and looked out over the land I'd bought.

Suddenly, Joanna made a noise that sounded like *Oh*, and went over to the picnic basket. She rummaged around in the bottom, then came back with a folded-up piece of paper, which she handed to me.

"The title to the land," she explained. "Jed gave it to me in the kitchen like you asked him to. There was another piece of paper with it," she continued. "I think you'll want to take a look."

I unfolded what she'd given me. The first page was the title. I glanced at it and set it aside. I looked at the second one. It appeared to be a hand-drawn map with a note at the top of it. I spread it out and read the note:

> *Friend—I don't know your name, but I reckon I'll learn it when we meet at the café. This here's to let you know I made me a*

hideout in them mountains at the back of the ranch. I got me some flour, a couple guns and some ammo, and some beans and vittles and such hid up there. I reckon you might need it some day. Jest foller the map below if'n you need it.

Jed

I stared at the map and looked up at the mountains in the distance. I could see the notch he had marked on the map clear enough. I passed it to Joanna. "Make sure you know how to find it," I told her. I moved to wake up Sarge. When Joanna was done with the map, I passed it to Sarge.

Sarge read the note, studied the map, and moved to pass it back to me.

"Keep it," I said. "When you get back to town, give it to Holt. Don't let nobody else get a look at it. If I get my back up against the wall, I'll need a few friends to know where I am."

Sarge nodded and tucked the page into his hat. He glanced overhead, then stood, walked over to his horse, and mounted up. "I'm gonna let you young 'uns have this place to yourselves," he announced with a grin. He tipped his hat to Joanna. "Jest about the best lunch I ever et." He chuckled, patting his belly. He put his heels to his horse and took the road to Silverton.

Joanna stood and pulled me to my feet. "Come

on," she said, keeping hold of my hand when I got up. "We haven't even seen the house yet. I want to see it."

We walked over to the front door. I can't say I've thought a lot about houses. I mean, a roof to keep the rain out and keep me warm in the winter, sure. I could see a chimney poking through the roof, so I wasn't too worried about the warm part. Joanna, though, stopped and looked for a long time before she was ready to move inside.

"Nice big porch, don't you think?" she asked.

I made sure to nod my head up and down. "Uh-huh."

"What do you think about those windows?" was the next question.

I stared hard at the windows and tried to think of something smart to say about the windows. I came up empty.

She shook her head and laughed. "Nice and wide, they'll let in plenty of morning sun and make the place bright." She shook her head again and pulled me toward the front door. "Let's take a look inside," she said.

I was on a little firmer ground inside. Joanna inspected the kitchen and said she was happy with it. I prowled around, inspecting the ceiling for leaks. I stopped to check the fireplace—it looked like somebody had built it who knew what they were doing.

"Oh. Come over here!" she called from around a corner.

She sounded pretty excited. I walked over and found her looking into a bedroom. There were two small bunks in opposite corners. I knew in a second the bedroom was for Jed's two kids. I joined Joanna and looked in.

Before I knew what was happening, she grabbed my shoulders and spun me around, pulled my head down, and laid one right on my lips. Right about then, I decided it had been a good idea to look at the house.

After a couple minutes that I don't recollect real clearly, we moved outside. Joanna pointed at a large garden at the side of the house. "Look, they had to leave the garden behind," she said.

We moved up and down the straight, well-tended rows. I glanced overhead. "Set it up for morning sun and afternoon shade," I said approvingly. "Too bad they had to leave all that hard work behind."

Joanna kneeled and pulled some carrots, radishes, and a little lettuce. "We can take some back," she murmured. She straightened up and saw me staring toward the notch at the foot of the mountains, out at the edge of my new ranch.

"You want to go out there and check out his hideout, don't you? The one he drew you a map of?" She moved over to stand beside me and looked out toward the notch. I just nodded a few times.

She took my arm and moved me out of the garden. "Let's go have a look at it," she said simply.

The hideout was right where he'd drawn it on the map, but I could see why he had drawn directions to it. It would have been hard to find otherwise. We had to lead the horses on foot up a trail that wound back into the mountains. The shale under our feet could be slippery at times. The steep cliffs shaded us as we climbed.

After five minutes of walking up the trail, we turned sharply left and saw a narrow cave entrance to our left. We tethered our horses on a log stretched between two large rocks. It seemed to have been set up there for that specific purpose.

We stepped inside the cave and paused to let our eyes adjust to the darkness. After a moment, I could see daylight filtering in from above at the back of the cave. We stepped to the back, and I peered up. There was a small hole in the ceiling. I looked down and saw the remnants of a small campfire on the floor of the cave. No doubt, I thought, the smoke from the fire drifted up through some brush above.

I stepped to a side wall and let out a low whistle. Joanna moved over to join me. There were sacks of dried beans, canned meat, some honey in a jar, a sack of flour, and a sack of sugar. I moved along the wall, staring at the food.

"He brought enough to feed his family," Joanna pointed out.

I nodded silently, then moved across to the other side. There was an old Sharps rifle leaning against the wall, as well as a Navy Colt revolver. They had stacked boxes of ammunition beside the guns.

We moved back toward the cave entrance. Four small mats were stashed against the wall. Something else leaning against the wall caught my attention, and I moved over to lift and carry it to the light of the entrance. It was an old cane pole with some fishing line and a hook.

"He thought of just about everything," I murmured to Joanna. "I wonder where he fished."

We stepped back outside, and I saw a flat rock, just about waist-high, giving a commanding view of the last fifty feet of the trail, as well as a good view of the valley below. I looked up and saw the cliff above me leaning slightly inward. Nobody could get a shot from above. It was an excellent defensive position.

Joanna took my hand, and we climbed upward to check the trail above us. After a few minutes, we heard rushing water. Around another curve, we found the trail flattened out beside a stream rushing down the mountain. In a pool in front of us, fat brown trout darted back and forth.

I turned and led her back down the trail. "It's just about as good a hideout as a man could have," I told her. "I'm glad to know about it, but we probably won't ever have to use it."

There's one thing I've noticed about myself. Sometimes, I'm good at guessing what's going to happen in my future. Sometimes I'm not.

Fred Moore leaned back in his chair at the brand-new sheriff's office and put his boots up on the desk. He put his hands behind his head and cut loose with a deep sigh of satisfaction. If he rolled his eyes down just a bit, he could see that big badge on his chest. He swung a glance around the office. It was still a little empty, but he could work on that.

Funny how this great offer for a new job had come out of nowhere. He'd been in a saloon down in Durango just a couple weeks ago, sucking down a beer and celebrating his release from the army. That army thing just hadn't agreed with him. Being in the army was harder work than he'd thought. A lot of marching around for nothing. When they'd made him a cook, that was alright with him. Now he was finally out.

The door to the saloon had opened, and Fred had seen somebody he knew. His sister's husband, in fact, Andy Knowles. Fred stared while Andy Knowles waved and walked across the saloon. He took a seat and signaled for another pitcher of beer.

Fred was still staring. "What're you doin' up here?" he finally asked. "I thought you was the mayor or something, down Silverton way."

Andy Knowles nodded, poured himself a beer, and leaned back. "That's right," he agreed. "Your sister told me you'd mustered out and were lookin' for work down here." He shot a glance over the beer glass. "That right?"

Fred recovered enough to pour himself another glass of beer. He didn't enjoy having his sister trying to take care of him. He wasn't a kid anymore. Twenty-three, he reminded himself. An army veteran, too. "I've got some job possibles," he announced.

Knowles nodded and set his beer glass on the table. "I'm sure you do," he agreed. He poured another glass and shot a keen glance across the table.

"You got any job possibles better than being the sheriff up in Silverton?"

Fred's hand froze in the air, halfway to the beer pitcher. His jaw dropped open again. He forced himself to look like he'd heard better offers. The truth was, he was about to take a job at the livery stables, forking hay and shoveling. He picked up the beer and stared at his brother-in-law. One thought still bothered him.

"I, uh," he said, stalling behind a cough. "I was in the army and all, but I haven't used a gun very much. Rifles, mainly, when I had to. What kind of town is Silverton?"

"Very calm town," Knowles lied smoothly. "Plus, I've got a guy there who can help you if there's any rough stuff. Name is Preacher. Great guy. You can meet him when you get to town."

A smile spread slowly across Fred's face as he relaxed and finished his beer, then reached for another. "Tell me more about it," he mumbled.

SIX

PREACHER'S ORDERS

T he door slammed loudly, jolting Fred Moore back to the present. He swung his gaze to the door. The words he'd thought about yelling at his rude visitor died on his lips. The man walking toward his desk was tall and thickly built. He wore a battered black hat and a Colt tied down on each hip. He shot a look at the sheriff, and Fred dropped his boots off the desk and sat up straight.

"Uh, can I help you?" Fred was trying for a deep, manly tone, but he was afraid this sounded more like a squeak.

The man sat down across the desk and stared at Fred for at least five seconds before growling his answer. "Yeah, mebbe you can hep me, but I think I kin hep you more. My name is Preacher Dalton."

Fred's stomach sunk to somewhere below his knees. His brother-in-law had described Preacher as a nice man who could help Fred clean up the rough edges around town. His gut told him this was the guy who would cause all the rough stuff around town. He licked his lips nervously and said nothing, staring at a spot on the wall just behind Preacher's ear.

Preacher looked around the room and saw the coffeepot in the corner. He stood, walked over, and poured himself a cup. After he'd tasted it, he swore, spat the coffee on the floor, and walked back over to take a seat.

Fred stared at the coffee on his floor. Funny, he thought, how dry his mouth had just gotten. He waited, trying to keep from looking scared. He had a feeling he wasn't fooling this guy. He knew he looked scared. His mind flashed back to the first day he'd gone to school in the little one-room building back home. There was a kid everybody called Moose. Moose always stood outside the school and took the food Fred's mom had given him for lunch. It had seemed like a pretty good trade to Fred, giving up his food and keeping his head on his shoulders.

"I'm gonna hep you clean up this here town," Preacher announced. "You don't have to do nuthin' but arrest the folks I tell you to."

Fred nodded. Were sheriffs supposed to do this? He didn't think so, but his gut told him to keep his mouth shut and keep nodding. He'd never gone wrong listening to his gut, he reminded himself.

Preached leaned back and thumped his muddy boots on the desk. "You been down to the Suds 'n Such Saloon?" he blurted.

Fred nodded and found his tongue. "Been there a time or two," he volunteered. "I, uh, had a couple beers." Fred liked the beer down there, but Preacher didn't need to hear that.

Preacher stared past him and finally nodded. "Gonna have to clean up that place," he announced. "Lotta trouble at that place." He stood and walked toward the door. "My boys and me will take care of it," he said over his shoulder. "You hear some trouble down there, you come down and arrest folks when I tell ya to."

The door clicked shut behind him. Fred stared at the door for a long time. He was feeling something in his gut again, and he knew what it was. It was fear. He wouldn't stand up against this Preacher guy—he knew that already. The only question was whether he should just get on his horse and ride out of town.

Preacher Dalton stalked toward the café in Silverton, shaking his head and muttering under his breath. "Useless," he mumbled to himself. As long as the kid would arrest the right people and do what Dalton wanted, he could live. Otherwise, Preacher wasn't above setting up the new sheriff as target number one in a gunfight. Might save him some trouble down the road.

He shoved open the café door, looking for the two new thugs Penfield was supposed to send to town. This was the third morning in a row he'd looked for them. Stopping inside the door and scanning the room, he saw what he was looking for.

There was a thickly built blonde kid with a lot of

muscles at a table in the corner and another one across the table, back to the wall. Penfield couldn't see his guns, but the guy on the other side of the table had to be the gunhand. These had to be Penfield's new guys. Preacher walked across, yanked out a chair, and parked himself at the table without a word.

"Uh, are you Preacher?" one of them asked.

"Yep." Preacher grabbed an empty coffee cup and waved it in the air until a waitress came across the room to fill it.

The kid that Preacher had figured to be the gunhand pointed across the table. "He's..."

"Don't care about the names," Preacher muttered. He pointed at the muscle man. "I'm calling you Blondie. And you..." He looked across the table. "I'm gonna call you Guns. Listen up. I'm gonna tell you what I want."

Preacher leaned in. "You're gonna bust up a saloon named Suds 'n Such. The owner runs the bar, and he keeps a shotgun underneath. Don't worry about that. I've got a guy gonna keep him outta this. You," he said, pointing at Blondie, "are gonna bust up a guy named Sarge. You'll know who he is. Just start a little rough stuff. He'll be the first one that comes over. He ain't big, but don't let that fool you. Take him down quick and hard."

Preacher turned to the gunhand. "A guy named Latigo Smith is gonna come in at some point. When he does, you kill him."

Guns, whose real name was Harv, blinked slowly several times. He picked up his coffee and took a long sip. "How'm I supposed to know who he is?"

Preacher jerked a thumb toward the street. "You kin find him at the bakery down the street. Go over there an' get yerself some coffee. He'll be in there makin' eyes at the girl that owns the place."

Harv stared out the window. "How good is he?"

Preacher shrugged. "Never saw him use his gun. You're supposed to be handy with them pistols, right? Just take him out. The sheriff'll do what I say later. You won't have no trouble in this town." He finished his coffee in one long slurp and left.

Harv and Blondie stayed at their table for a long time and stared at each other.

"I don't mind bustin' up a guy a little," Blondie announced. "How 'bout you, though, Harv? You gonna gun down this Latigo Smith guy?"

Harv took a long sip from his coffee cup and stared out the window. He shrugged. "Mebbe if I can make it look like he had a fair chance. I don't mind doin' it that way. And if the sheriff will really go along with this, yeah." He drummed his fingers on the tabletop nervously. "Penfield promised real good money," he mumbled.

Harv made his decision and stood. "Let's go to the bakery and see what this Smith guy looks like."

I liked it when things slowed down after the morning rush at the bakery. Joanna could make some breakfast for the both of us and come to join me at the table. I always timed it so I could get here when things slowed down. Today, I thought as I tied into my eggs, was starting out just right.

Joanna brought two steaming mugs of coffee and smiled as she took a seat across from me. "You going back out to your new ranch today?" she asked.

I nodded. "First thing after we finish eating," I told her. "I want to check the upper pasture to see how many head of cattle got left behind and what kind of shape they're in. Then I—"

The sound of the bell interrupted me at the front door, and two more customers came in. Joanna got up and went behind the counter to serve them. I glanced over the top of my coffee mug and got the funny feeling these guys were staring at me. They looked like they were sizing me up, I thought. I stared back, and they went up to the counter. Joanna gave them both a mug of coffee, then returned to the table while they parked at a table across the room.

I glanced over at them. One was blonde and big, with a lot of muscles on him. Kinda like Otis, I thought, the guy I'd fought with out in the street the other day. The other one was smaller, kinda narrow across the shoulders. He wore a gun and seemed to avoid looking at me now.

After ten minutes, they left without looking back at me. Joanna stared after them as they closed the door and walked across the street.

"They were really looking at you when they came in," she murmured.

I nodded. "Yep. I thought so too." I stared out the

window and shrugged. "If they've got a beef with me, I'll know soon enough, I guess."

Joanna frowned and opened her mouth to answer me when the bell on the front door rang again. She got up to wait on the new customer. I growled under my breath while I finished my breakfast. For the slowest time of day, it was downright busy in here.

━━━

Harv and Blondie stopped about a block down from the bakery. Harv dug into his pocket, produced a cigar, and lit it up.

Blondie watched. "You gonna do it?" he asked.

Harv puffed thoughtfully. "Yeah. He might be pretty salty. I'll get the drop on him, though. Didn't nobody say it had to be a fair fight." He looked at the sun overhead and scowled. "Saloon ain't open yet," he mumbled. He took some more puffs on his cigar and started down the street toward the boardinghouse. "C'mon," he drawled. "I got some whiskey in the room."

━━━

The new customer at Joanna's Bakery got his coffee and brought it over to my table. Joanna stood behind him.

"Latigo Smith," she said, pointing at me, "this is our new sheriff, Fred Moore."

Surprised, I looked up, blinked several times, and pointed at an empty chair. This guy, I thought, looked even less like a sheriff than Andrew Knowles had looked like a mayor. Matter of fact, I thought to myself, this kid was in for a rough ride as sheriff of a mining boomtown. There was something strange about the folks getting into office around here...

I put the last mouthful of breakfast where it goes and leaned back with my coffee. I hardly knew what to say to this kid.

"How long you been sheriff?" I asked. I had a feeling his appointment was real recent.

He grinned, looking pretty sheepish. "Just got into town yesterday," he admitted. "I'm just tryin' to get acquainted with the folks I need to know."

I nodded, fishing for something else to say. I couldn't think of much.

"You got a business in town?" he asked. I had a funny feeling he knew the answer already. Or thought he knew the answer.

"Yep," I said, studying his reaction to that. Just like I thought, his eyebrows climbed way up his head.

I took a big slurp of my coffee and grinned at Joanna. He crawfished around on his chair, waitin' for me to explain. I didn't help. Finally, he couldn't stand it.

"Where, er, what...is your business?" he finally asked.

"I'm part owner of the Suds 'n Such Saloon," I told him.

His eyebrows climbed up his forehead again. "Oh...I, uh, I thought somebody named Holt owned that saloon."

I nodded. "We're partners," I agreed. "Holt runs it.

I come in ever' now and then and help out if there's a problem, or if there's somethin' he just needs my help with. I own a ranch outside of town, too. I'll be spending a lot of time out there."

He stayed for another ten minutes and we talked, but nuthin' got said, if you know what I mean. I could see his brain had gone to work, sorting out what I'd told him. Somebody had talked to him about me, that was for sure. He hadn't been thinkin' he was going to meet a business owner and respectable rancher.

Finally, he stood, put his hat back on, and tipped his hat to Joanna. "Ma'am," he said. He nodded at me and left.

Fred Moore stood outside the bakery for a minute. He was feeling worse about his job and this town every hour that went by, it seemed like. Latigo Smith didn't seem like a troublemaker or a guy he wanted to arrest. What else had his brother-in-law and Preacher told him that wasn't true?

"Sheriff!" Moore froze in his tracks. He knew that voice. He'd heard it just this morning. He turned around, looking for that battered black hat. He didn't have to look very far. The guy who called himself Preacher was walking toward him.

Preacher looked past Moore at the bakery, then came to a stop, still staring at the bakery. "You bin in there?" he demanded.

Moore nodded. "Yes, I went in to meet the bakery owner. Mr. Latigo Smith was in there as well."

Preacher's head jerked around and he gave Moore a hard stare. "Smith is trouble," he snarled. "He's part of what you come to town to clean up. Him and that saloon owner. Maybe even that girl that owns the bakery."

"Smith told me he owns part of the saloon," Moore mumbled. He hated that his voice sounded like a squeak again.

Preacher took another step in. Moore could smell the whiskey and stale cigar smoke. He took a step back. Preacher stepped in again and pointed at two guys leaning up against the wall of the general store across the street.

"You see them two guys?" he rasped. Moore nodded.

"Them two guys might pay a visit to that saloon to, uh, clean some things up. There might be a little dust-up down there. Them two guys," he rumbled, "don't get theirselves arrested. That clear? You might wanna arrest that guy Holt that owns the saloon and that Latigo Smith feller, too, if'n they make trouble."

Preacher stayed there in Moore's face, glaring at him.

Moore swallowed a few times and nodded. Preacher left and went across the street to join the two thugs leaning against the wall of the general store.

Moore continued down to the sheriff's office, went inside, and sat heavily in his chair. He stared at the desktop and thought about the morning he'd had. He wasn't sure he had the courage to defy this guy, Preacher. Maybe, he thought, he would need to get out

of this town. The job at the livery stable in Durango
didn't sound too bad right now.

I found only a half-dozen head of cattle left behind at
the ranch, but I got a good look at the property while I
explored the northern ends of the grazing pasture and
worked a couple draws near the stream cutting across
the western side. The cattle looked to be in good
shape. I rounded them up and drifted them to a fenced
pasture, lower down and closer to the house.

I was even happier with the ranch now that I'd had
a chance to look it over. The railroad ran through just
off to the west. I could hear the whistle and catch a
little rumble from the tracks when I got closer to the
railroad. I pulled up and listened for a moment,
wondering if Penfield had wanted this ranch so much
because it was close to the railroad tracks. It was something to think about.

When I had the cattle settled down, I came back to
the house. There was a tool shed behind the garden. I
pried the door open and glanced inside. Jed had left a
lot behind here, leaving in a hurry the way he had.
There were hammers, a couple hoes, and an axe
stacked neatly in a corner. I shook my head. He'd tried
to make a life for his family here. At least I'd given
him a fair price and seen him off to start again.

I went back inside the house and wandered
around, picturing what this might look like after I'd
had a chance to settle in. Pausing at the door to the
kid's room, I remembered the smile it put on Joanna's

face when she'd seen this. That got me decided it was time to go back to town.

Riding up Main Street, I decided there was time enough to stop off at the bakery. She'd be closing up by now and I might get put to work, but I'd never been afraid of doing some work.

I dismounted and had started toward the door when I heard somebody calling my name. I turned and saw a young redheaded kid named Herbie, whom Holt paid to do a little work in the kitchen sometimes, washing dishes mainly.

Herbie was coming on at a good speed, yelling my name and waving his arms in the air. My gut told me this was trouble. My hand dropped automatically to check the Colt in my gun belt.

Herbie skidded to a stop in front of me, his eyes as big as silver dollars and his breath coming in gasps. "You got to come to the saloon," he burst out, gasping between breaths. "They've done busted up Sarge, an' they're holdin' a gun on Mr. Holt! You got to git down there now!"

I broke into a trot behind Herbie, heading down to the Suds 'n Such. The bakery door opened behind me and I heard a yell from Joanna.

"Lat, where are you going?"

I waved a hand and looked back over my shoulder. "Stay here!" I shouted. "I'll be back!"

I could hear shouting and commotion as we reached the saloon.

SEVEN
CHALLENGED

I t had all started out pretty slowly, at least as far as Holt was concerned. This was a pretty normal night at the saloon, starting out pretty slowly but picking up as more miners came in and ordered. A couple of friendly card games started in the middle of the room.

Minutes later, a couple guys came in that Holt hadn't seen before. One was blonde and full of muscles. The other was smaller and wore a gun. That wasn't too unusual, so he wasn't too worried about the gun. The one with the gun drifted over to a card table. The guy with the muscles sat at a table in the corner, kept to himself, and ordered a beer. Holt stopped watching them and got busy keeping up with the orders at the bar. He had Sarge to keep an eye on things out there.

A few minutes later, things started getting a little rowdier at the table where the new guy with the gun was gambling. Holt swung around to take a look. The new guy was still in his seat, raking in a pile of money. The guy across the table was shouting at him, telling the new guy he was a cheat. Players scattered away from the table.

Holt moved toward the bar and the shotgun he had lying on the shelf right below it. He didn't reach it before a familiar face showed up right in front of him. It was the same guy who'd held a gun on him the night Preacher Dalton stirred up trouble in the saloon. The man dropped his hand to rest on his pistol and shook his head at Holt.

Now, both guys were standing out there, facing each other across the card table. Holt saw Sarge charging across the room, yelling at everybody to stay calm. Both card players seemed to freeze where they were, but the other stranger, the guy with the muscles, moved across the room, surprisingly fast for such a big guy. He grabbed Sarge by the collar and the seat of his pants, then threw him across the room. A table crashed to the ground and the big stranger moved in after Sarge.

Holt turned his head slightly and caught the eye of a kid named Herbie, who washed dishes and cleaned up in the kitchen for him. Holt mouthed the word *Lat* and cut his eyes toward the door. Herbie nodded and dashed outside.

———

This was going about as well as Harv could have hoped. Preacher's other gunman had the barkeep covered, meaning Harv wouldn't be soaking up a shotgun blast. Blondie had thrown the guy they called Sarge across the room. Blondie moved in to finish him off.

Harv turned slightly toward the door, just enough to get off a clean shot at Latigo Smith if he came in. He was ready without being obvious. Maybe the guy wouldn't even come.

Blondie yanked Sarge off the floor and delivered a punishing blow to the kidneys. Sarge moaned and leaned over. Blondie swung a huge fist into Sarge's face. Fascinated, Harv watched as Sarge crumpled to the floor. He glanced sideways at the bar. Preacher's gunman still had things under control.

Harv's stomach lurched when he realized he hadn't kept a close watch on the front door. The quiet voice from the doorway caught him by surprise.

"Everybody back up and keep your hands where I can see 'em."

It was Latigo Smith, one quick look told him there was no doubt about it. Harv had seen him just that morning at the bakery. In the next instant, Harv knew Smith hadn't drawn his gun. A slight smile spread across his face. Why hadn't this fool come in with his gun drawn?

Harv's hand dropped to his gun, and he began his draw. It was the last thing he would remember.

━━

I came through the front door, not sure what to expect. A sweep of the room showed me Sarge on the floor, crumpled up. The blonde guy I'd seen in the bakery this morning was standing over him. Obviously, he was the one who'd done this to Sarge.

I cut my eyes to the right. Preacher's gunhand, the one Sarge had knocked out with his pistol just the other day, was standing at the bar, covering Holt just like he had before, keeping Holt away from his shotgun.

It only took another second to see that Preacher Dalton wasn't in here. That was a relief. Then something else registered at the corner of my vision. There was somebody else over there—it was the other guy from the bakery. His hand dropped to his gun.

My Colt came up easily, and I aimed for the center of his chest. Both shots hit where I'd aimed them—the first in the center of his chest and the other straight through his heart. He fell over the table behind him. Money and cards flew in the air as he slid to the floor and the table came to rest on top of him.

The sound of the shots echoed for just a moment and then it got deathly quiet in there. I swung my gun to cover the guy in front of the bar. His hand was on his gun. It was about half-drawn.

"This is the second time you've caused me trouble," I growled at him. "Go ahead and haul that hogleg if you've a mind to. Might as well dig two graves instead of one."

He shook his head and stood frozen, his eyes shooting hatred at me.

"You don't wanna die tonight, then just finish pulling that pistol, only real slow. Lay it on the bar and get out."

He did like he was told. I moved over to check on

Sarge. The blonde guy who'd worked him over backed off to stand against the wall. His eyes were glittering at me too. I didn't seem to be real popular in here.

Sarge struggled to his feet and collapsed into a chair with a moan. I swung to look at one of the miners near the card table. "Get the doc," I barked. He left.

The front door swung open, and I wheeled around to see Fred Moore, the new sheriff, followed by Preacher Dalton. Dalton pointed a finger at me. "There's the guy you want!" he hollered at Moore. "Take him in!"

Moore had a gun, but he left it in his belt. He pulled an old pair of shackles from his pocket and moved toward me.

One by one, I saw miners and a few cowhands moving in, circling me to stop the sheriff from getting to me. A couple of the miners picked up boards from the shattered tables.

"Other guy hauled iron fust," one of them growled. "Seen it plain as day." Others nodded and moved in closer.

Moore looked at the miner who'd spoken—a huge, red-haired man with a bushy beard, holding a slat from one of the tables in his huge paws. Moore stopped short, looking like he'd rather be anywhere else. He glanced backward at Preacher Dalton, who cut loose with a heartfelt oath and stomped out the door.

The sheriff put the shackles back in his pocket and turned to go.

"Hey!" I was pointing at the blonde guy with the

muscles leaning up against the side wall. "He busted up Sarge over here. Ain't you gonna take him in?"

Moore looked at me, looked at the blonde guy, then stared at the floor and shook his head. "Nope," he said slowly. "Everybody just...get this place cleaned up." He swung a hand at all the wrecked tables on the floor, then pointed at the corpse. "Get him over to whoever you've got around here to take care of dead guys." He turned and shuffled out the door, followed by the blonde stranger who had taken Sarge apart.

When I looked in on Sarge at the doc's office, he didn't look like the same guy I'd known. He had some kind of bandage wrapped around his ribs and another one around his head. His face was already turning a kind of purple color, and it was hard to understand him when he talked.

He waved me into a seat next to the bed. "Doc just left," he said, kinda slurring the words. "He says I'm all stove up."

I ignored the joke and took a seat. He looked even worse when I got close-up like this.

"What does he say is wrong?" I asked.

He shrugged and stared down at his chest. "Busted ribs, mebbe three or four. All of 'em hurt. Kinda hard to tell how many." He pointed at his face. "Busted jaw, too. Gotta eat a lot of scrambled eggs for a while." He turned his head slowly to look at me.

"Who was those two that done this stuff?" he growled. "Some of Preacher Dalton's guys, I know, but

I ain't never see either of 'em before. That big guy, he caught me by surprise. I think he had a mind to put his boots to me on the ground before you come in."

"Yeah, Preacher's guys," I agreed. "Saw them in the bakery this morning. Partners, I guess. I saw the blonde guy across the street outside the saloon just now. I told him to get the first train outta town tomorrow or I'll put him on Boot Hill next to his buddy."

Sarge laughed, then coughed, then grabbed his ribs. "Wish I could've seen that," he chuckled. Then he turned serious and motioned me to lean in closer.

"This is way bigger than fights in the Suds 'n Such," he whispered, looking around the room. "You got to watch yore step and be careful. You an' Holt both." He lifted the corner of his pillow and I saw his old Navy Colt just beneath the pillow. "There's folks wanna take us out."

I nodded. "That guy might not leave if Preacher's backing his plays. What folks, all of 'em, I mean?" I asked, thinking things over. "Preacher Dalton? Ike Penfield? And how do you know this?"

He nodded slowly. "Both them guys you mentioned," he agreed. "Likely it's Penfield callin' the shots. He's a big man down in Leadville, you know. Lots of money from saloons and gamblin'. Got the money by robbing miners, that's what I heard."

I leaned in. "Who told you this?"

Sarge reached out to get a drink from a glass of water next to his bed. I took the glass when he was done and put it back on the stand. He moved a little to get a better position, moaned, then lay still. He looked around again.

"I bin talkin' to the miners when they come in the saloon," he muttered. "They're just small timers, doin' some panning for the most part, finding just enough color to make it worth their while. Thing is, a lot of 'em been robbed on their way to town with the gold. Highwaymen, mebbe all from the same bunch, take their money and jest disappear back into the hills."

"Who's behind it?" I demanded. "They know who's doing this?"

"Penfield," Sarge whispered. "They think it's Penfield. He's got so much money. Jest about owns the town in Leadville. They think he's comin' here, too. Wants to take over this place. You're standin' in his way. That means you got to watch yore step."

Sarge coughed and laid back on his pillow while I thought that one over.

"Who've you talked to? Among the miners, I mean. Do I know any of 'em?"

"You kinda do," Sarge grinned. "That big redhead that stepped up and threatened to mash the sheriff's hat in. His name is Dugan. He's been in town for a couple days. Finally got some nuggets past the robbers and wanted to hang around in town a little. He'll tell you most of what you need to know."

He laid back on the pillow again, then sat back up. "Jest be careful," he warned me again. "They're watchin' you. They don't want you getting in the way."

I sat back and stared out the window. "What can

we do to stop this?" I asked. "You must have thought about that. What would hurt them the most?"

"Stop that gang of highwaymen," Sarge advised. "Take away the money. That'll hit 'em right in their money belts."

"Right." I patted his shoulder. "You let the doc take care of you. Try not to be an ornery old coot like usual for a while." I turned to go.

"Lat," he said. I turned back to look at him.

"Don't get it all cleaned up afore I'm outta this place," he muttered. "I want in on this. It's plumb personal now."

I nodded and left the doctor's office.

Fred Moore was pacing around the sheriff's office, mostly because he couldn't sit still this morning. He hadn't been able to sleep last night either, but he'd come to a decision, and he was strangely excited about it. Preacher Dalton would be in here to see him, there was no doubt about that. Fred had decided to stand up to Preacher this morning.

He didn't plan on shooting it out with the man. That would be suicide. He'd barely handled a pistol, and Preacher was said to be an expert. What he'd decided was to stop doing what Preacher told him to do. Moore glanced around the corner and down the hallway. His bags were all packed, and he knew what time the train left this morning. First, though, he was going to do something he'd never done before. He was going to stand up for himself and do the right thing.

Moore flinched only a little when he heard the door open, then slam shut behind him. He saw the battered black hat first, then saw Preacher turning around. "Where is he? In the cells? Where's Latigo Smith?" Preacher barked.

Moore had been sure not to wear a gun this morning. He couldn't give Preacher an excuse. He forced himself to walk calmly over to his desk and take a seat. He forced himself to return Preacher's stare and to speak evenly. No squeaking this morning, he'd promised himself that.

"I don't have him. Didn't arrest him. Several witnesses said he did nothing but defend himself."

Preacher's mouth opened and closed twice. A red flush crept up his neck. He crossed to the desk and leaned over it. "What did you say?"

Moore didn't blink. He repeated himself. "He defended himself against a guy who started a fight by cheating at cards. I didn't arrest Smith. Won't be arresting him this morning, either." He reached up slowly and removed the badge from his chest, placing it carefully on the desk. "I guess you'll be wanting that," he said.

The rage on Preacher's face turned to confusion. It didn't seem like he could just shoot this guy—he was the mayor's brother-in-law, after all. The miners in the bar had surrounded Smith last night. It could get pretty ugly to haul Smith in right now, anyway. Preacher stared at Fred Moore again, and he leaned in a little closer.

"Git outta town," he snarled.

Moore nodded and stood slowly. "Already packed

up," he told Preacher. "I'll be on the morning train out." He stood his ground and stared until Preacher turned and moved for the door. Only after it slammed shut did he heave a sigh of relief.

Moore walked over, picked up his bags, and let himself out of the sheriff's office, closing it gently behind him. He started walking toward the rail station. He'd heard California was a good place to go these days. He would head out there.

As he walked, he felt relief wash over him. He felt something else too, something he hadn't felt in a long time. He felt proud of himself.

I stopped at the Suds 'n Such Saloon first thing in the morning. I knew Holt would already be there, cleaning up whatever needed to be cleaned after last night's shooting and fight. I found him there, just like I'd expected.

The place looked better than I thought it would. Somebody had hauled the broken tables away. The corpse was gone. I found Holt mopping the floor. I walked over to take a look. The bloodstain was mostly gone. We could put a table over that spot.

Holt put the mop bucket away and walked over to sit on a stool at the bar with me. He looked around and shook his head. "Not too much damage from last night," he said. "I just wonder if they're gonna keep comin' after us here."

I wished I had better news for him, but I knew he needed the truth more than anything. I shook my head. "You can keep tryin'," I said, "but I think some-body wants this place closed. Somebody with some money behind him." I looked up at him. "Sarge thinks it's a guy named Ike Penfield. Runs a big gambling and highwayman operation out of Leadville. Maybe he wants to take over Silverton, too."

Holt slumped down on his stool a little. "What can we do about it?"

"Sarge had an idea," I said. "A good idea. He thinks we should go after the guys stealing ore and money from the miners. He thinks that's where most of Penfield's money comes from. Hit 'em where it hurts. Do you know that guy named Dugan, the redhead that stepped up for me last night?"

Holt brightened a little. "Shore do. One of my best customers."

"I need to talk to him," I said. "Not here, though. Out at the ranch. Can you give him directions and send him out my way?"

"You got it, pard." He looked around the saloon. "You gonna need me out there? Mebbe in that hide-away Sarge told me about?"

"Maybe," I said. "You can just give it another try here for a few days. If those boys come back, you could shut 'er down for a while here and come out." The next part was the part that had me scared. "Maybe Joanna, too," I admitted. "She might have to close down, too. I'm goin' to see her next."

I stepped out of the saloon and headed down Main Street. The first thing I saw was Fred Moore, carrying a canvas bag. As he got closer, I saw he wasn't wearing his badge.

I stared at the bag he was carrying. "Goin' some-where?" I asked.

He nodded and pointed down the street. "Catching the morning train," he said. "Going to California, I think." He looked both ways and leaned in a little. "Preacher Dalton wanted you brought in and I wouldn't do it. Watch yourself."

"Who's behind Preacher Dalton?" I asked. "He's a thug—he ain't got the smarts to run this whole thing."

Moore scowled and stared down the street. "You know my brother-in-law, Knowles, the mayor around here?"

That surprised me. "I've met Knowles," I said. "I didn't know he was your brother-in-law."

"He is," Moore answered. "I'm pretty sure his cousin, a guy named Ike Penfield, is behind all this. You know Penfield?"

"Heard of him," I answered. "Didn't know the part about being cousin to the mayor in town."

Moore picked up his bag and patted my shoulder. "He is. Watch yourself." He headed on down to the train station. It was the last time I saw him.

EIGHT
HIT 'EM WHERE IT HURTS

I ke Penfield stood by the window of his store office, as he thought of it, in Leadville. He was expecting a visit from his other lieutenant—the one besides Preacher Dalton. Preacher ran things in town and handled the gunmen if he needed to. Right now, Preacher was up in Silverton, getting things ready for Penfield to move up there.

The other half of Penfield's operation was the one that had gotten him started and made the money he'd needed to take over towns like Leadville and Silverton. Ever since they'd hit what was named the Smuggler Vein, the gold and silver had been flowing out of those hills north and west of here. Most of that ore had been in the hands of small-time placer miners and panners until they tried to bring it to town. That was where Deuce Thorne and his boys came into the picture.

Penfield half-grinned to himself, still staring out the window and waiting for Thorne to show up.

Thorne had always hated that nickname, Deuce. Now Penfield chuckled. The man was bad at poker, but good at robbing miners. Penfield had no intention of calling him anything but Deuce. He glanced at the clock in the corner with irritation. The man was late. Penfield hated that, no matter how far he made them ride for a meeting with him.

Deuce Thorne and his gang of five worked one of two passes, mainly. Both offered significant chances to rob a miner or small group of miners as they worked their way along narrow mountain trails, trying to get to the rails in Silverton.

One trail was called the Hardrock Hundred Trail. The trail came in from the west, connecting with Silverton or mining settlements around Silverton. The other one was called the Ice Lake Basin Trail, running from Ice Lake, again mainly west of Silverton. It ran through several mining camps on the way to town. The spoils to be had were large on both trails. Thorne's gang worked back and forth between the two trails, robbing whoever wasn't armed or paying guards for protection. Once in a while, the gang ventured a little farther out and worked the Animas Forks Trail. As long as they kept hitting pay dirt with the robberies, Penfield didn't really care where they did their job.

The trick was to not bring too much gold and silver to the trains all at once. They would raise suspicions. So, most of the loot had been stored in an abandoned mine at Ice Lake, on the far end of the trail to Silverton. That was what Penfield needed to talk to Deuce Thorne about today. He wanted a little of the loot moved to the railroad here in Leadville. It was time to cash in a little more. From here, Penfield could move it out to California and get his money. Those boys at the railroad didn't raise their eyebrows too much if the boxes were small and not too heavy.

Penfield expected an argument from Deuce about this, as always, but he was ready for it. Deuce and his boys made too much money to raise too big a fuss. If they did, well, Penfield would have another job for Preacher to take of. Pretty sweet setup, that was how Penfield thought of it.

The door of the office opened and closed suddenly, causing Penfield to jump and whirl to his left. His hand dropped to his gun belt, then he relaxed. It was Deuce Thorne, but he hadn't used the trail through the woods at the back. He must have come down the alley from Main Street, out front, and then along the back of the building. Penfield smoothed the scowl on his face. He didn't want Deuce to have the satisfaction of knowing he'd startled Penfield.

The smirk on Deuce Thorn's face died away as Penfield stared at him. He moved to take the seat Penfield pointed at, then sat and waited. Penfield always liked to do the talking, Deuce had learned that much in the last year.

Thorne was just settling in his chair when Penfield dropped into the desk chair across from him. "Time to move some loot," Penfield blurted.

Thorne nodded, he had been expecting that. "Silverton," he answered. It wasn't a question, it was a statement—they had argued about this before.

"Not Silverton. Leadville," Penfield said flatly. His

stare across the desk challenged Deuce to argue with him.

Deuce Thorne smoothed his beard. His mind was racing. He decided to weigh in and argue about this. Penfield needed the money Deuce and his boy were bringing in. "We kin get the loot to Silverton in less'n one day," he reminded Penfield, ignoring the harsh glare he was getting. "Takes two days an' then some to git it to Leadville. We might even git robbed ourselves, one 'o these days, gittin it down here to Leadville."

Penfield continued his stare, shaking his head. "Still too dangerous up there," he barked. "Ain't got control of that town yet. Leadville. Right down here, just like before." Reading the look in Thorne's eyes, Penfield decided to throw him a bone.

"You'll get paid right after you load it on the train, just like always," Penfield pointed out. He paused. "I'll pay extra this time. Thirty dollars for all you boys, instead of twenty dollars, right after the train leaves town."

The look in Thorne's eyes told Penfield greed had won out. Thorne would try one more time, but Penfield was waiting with the answer.

"Thirty for all my boys, but what about me? I done all the hirin' and taken all the risks. What're you gonna pay me?"

"You don't have to tell 'em I'm givin' you thirty apiece," Penfield pointed out. "Give 'em twenty-five and keep the rest. It's still more money for them, and they ain't never gonna know the difference."

Deuce blinked a few times, then nodded and stood. "We'll git right on it. Be back in a few days for the money," he muttered. The door closed softly behind him.

Penfield reached for a cigar, lit it, and shook his head. Why hadn't the man ever thought of shorting his gang on the money? It's the first thing Penfield would have done. That, he thought, is why he was running this operation.

▬

Joanna had ridden out to the ranch this morning to join me for the meeting with Dugan. We had argued about this last night. I didn't want her involved in this, but Joanna, I reminded myself, was a strong-minded woman. Despite my worries, I kept looking out the window, excited about her coming back out to the ranch.

I heard the hoofbeats before I saw her buckskin mare coming around the corner. I hurried outside, swung her down off the horse, and she rewarded me with a kiss for my efforts. We went into the house. Joanna swept a critical eye around the front room and pulled three chairs together, clearly planning to join the conversation.

I watched, wondering if I could keep her out of harm's way if the bullets flew. I decided he wanted to change the subject.

"Did you just hang the Closed sign in the bakery door?" I asked. "Will anybody be suspicious or try to follow?"

"Nobody followed," she assured me. "I put another sign with the Closed sign. It says *Gone for*

Supplies." She patted my hand. "I'm sure they know I need to get flour and sugar and so on every once in a while."

I grumbled, nodded, and sat in one of the chairs. Joanna took a seat next to me. We waited in silence. When more hoofbeats sounded on the trail outside, I hurried out to meet Dugan and showed him into the front room.

I was a little worried about Dugan's manners and how he would react to Joanna's presence, but I didn't need to. Big and powerful with flowing, uncombed red hair, Dugan surprised both of them by leaning over to kiss Joanna's hand.

"Ma'am," he said, removing his hat and taking a seat.

We got down to business in a hurry. "There's about fifteen miners I know that've been robbed out there," Dugan said shortly. "I'm sure there's more, but those are the ones I know. We're ready to do somethin' about it." His eyes dropped to the Colt at my waist. "We got rifles," he said. "Mostly some old Sharps and a couple Winchester '73s. We kin shoot the rifles. Not too good with them hoglegs," he said, pointing at the Colt.

I exchanged glances with Joanna. "Let's back up a little," I said. "Where are you boys getting robbed? I know it's when you bring the dust and ore into town, but what trails are you using?"

"Ice Lake Basin Trail," Dugan answered instantly. "That's the one me and my friends use, anyway. I heard tell some fellers was robbed over on the Hardrock Hunnerd Trail. I ain't never used that one.

Mebbe there's folks been robbed on some other trails, too."

I grabbed a pencil and a piece of paper. Joanna reached out, took them, and started making notes. Good, I thought, I can't read my own writing about half the time, anyway. I glanced at the notes and looked back at Dugan.

"Do you know if they take the stolen ore to town right away? And how many do you think there are in the gang?"

"Five, mebbe six." Dugan stared at the floor. "One of 'em stands out in the trail an' holds a shotgun on us, but there's more of 'em up there in the rocks where I ain't got a shot at 'em." He nodded. "I think five."

"Do you they take it on into town?" I prodded. "It would be hard to take it all in right away. It's a pretty heavy load. Any idea about that?"

Dugan scratched his beard and furrowed up his forehead. Finally, he shook his head back and forth. "Jest dunno," he admitted. "They stayed where they was, and held them guns on me till I rode away."

"That's okay." I was only a little disappointed. If they were hiding the stuff somewhere, it was unlikely anybody would have seen it. I thought about it a little more. "What about hiding places along the trail?" I asked. "Are there places where they could stash some of that gold and silver until they're ready to move it?"

Dugan went back to scratching his beard and staring at the floor. "Yeah, I'd say there's probly several spots along them trails," he muttered. "There's some natural caves in them cliff walls in places. Plus, sometimes the boys use their pickaxes, digging into the cliff walls to foller one 'o them quartz veins. When the quartz plays out, it leaves a little cave. Mebbe a big cave if the vein was big enough. You want I should scout some of them out?"

I shook my head. "Too dangerous," I told him. "They'll be watching you after you stood up to 'em when they tried to come after me the other night in the saloon. Give me some time. I'll do the scouting." I looked over at Joanna. She was still making a few notes.

"Do you know how far that Ice Lake Basin Trail goes?" I asked. "Clear back to the lake, I guess?"

Dugan nodded. "That's what they tell me. Trail peters out somewhere around Ice Lake. Never been that far down the trail, myself. I know some of the boys done some diggin' up that way, though."

"Okay," I said. "I'll do some scouting. Give me several days. I'll try to find their ambush spots and maybe if they've stored some loot."

Dugan leaned forward impatiently. "Whaddya want me to do?" he demanded.

Another thought struck me. "These guys have robbed you on the Ice Lake Basin Trail, right?" I asked.

Dugan scowled and nodded. "Yup. They taken about a month's worth of work, too."

I reached for the pencil and pad of paper. Joanna handed it to me. "Draw the trail and the spot where they held you up, best as you can."

Dugan spent several minutes drawing the spot and described it to me until I felt pretty sure I could find it. I tucked the paper away in my pocket.

"One more thing," I said. "I need you to find out

who else has been robbed and where it's happened lately." I answered. "If I know where they struck last and how long it's been, it'll give me a better idea what happens next."

Dugan nodded with satisfaction. "I'll find out. I'll ask the boys down at the Suds 'n Such over the next couple days." A grin creased his face. "You think they'll send Blondie Boy after me like they done Sarge? He won't eat right for a month if he comes after me."

I thought about that ham-sized fist crashing into somebody's jaw and winced. "Keep an eye out," I agreed. "But they might use a gun on you. Be real careful. Can you come back this way in maybe four days?"

"Four days. You got it, boss." He held out that huge paw of his and I reached out for a handshake. Dugan left, and I stood there for a minute, massaging my hand.

Joanna looked at me and laughed. "Maybe don't shake his hand next time," she advised.

We stood outside, listening to the hoofbeats moving down the trail as Dugan rode back to Silverton. Joanna linked her arm through mine.

"I saw Sarge this morning before I rode out," she told me. "He's pretty lucky. Doc says his jaw isn't broken. Just three ribs. Sarge wants to just wrap 'em up and ride out here. Doc told him to stay in bed until the end of the week."

I chuckled. "Good luck keeping him down," I said. "See if you can get him to stay put for a few days. Tell him he can ride out here and hole up in the hideout up there in the hills." I lifted my eyes up toward the notch in the mountains at the edge of the property.

Joanna moved toward her buckskin. "Holt says he'll stick it out as long as he can, but he's thinking he'll be out here, too." She swung aboard the buckskin.

"What about you?" I asked. "They might not do anything to a woman, but they might. Don't take any chances."

"I won't," she promised, leaning over to give me a kiss. "I'm likely to be out here before long, too. I won't let anybody follow me." With that, she put her boots to the buckskin and followed Dugan down the trail back to Silverton.

I packed enough grub and ammo for a week, but I didn't think it would take me that long. I wouldn't be able to ride the trail all the way to Ice Lake this time. Dugan would meet me before then. Plus, I had a feeling Holt wouldn't be able to stay in business for even a week.

The first day didn't tell me much. The trail was narrow and winding, just like Dugan had said, but I didn't really see any good ambush spots. I pulled over as the sun was dipping down in the west and looked at Dugan's map. I hadn't reached the spot he'd marked yet.

I hobbled my horse and gave him a bag of feed, then made a small fire to cook some beans and biscuits Joanna had given me earlier. I rolled up in the blankets, wondering if Penfield's gang was somewhere in these hills with me.

Sunup found me back on the trail. I'd hoped to pass a miner or two on his way to town, but that wasn't in the cards. I saw nobody else on the trail, and the tracks I saw were several days old.

When the sun was getting high overhead, I saw a place that looked like a possible holdup spot. The trail widened out a little, and there were two peaks nearby that offered a pretty good field of fire down on the trail. I checked the map—this wasn't where they had robbed Dugan, but it was worth checking out.

Leading my horse off the trail, I climbed up the first of the two peaks on foot and looked for tracks. I found some. I was guessing two guys had stood here and maybe kneeled, using boulders to steady their rifles while they aimed down on the trail.

I climbed to the second spot and found more tracks. Searching in the brush nearby, I found two rifle shells. It looked like somebody had put up a little resistance down there on the trail.

Stopping to mark this spot on the map, I remounted and kept pushing north and west. The spot they had used to hold up Dugan couldn't be too far from here. Less than two hours later, I found it. This one was even better than the first one, if you were out to bushwhack a man and steal his gold.

The trail descended here into a bowl before climbing sharply up. Peaks on three sides gave a clear shot down on the trail, and there were trees and bushes by the side of the trail on one side. They gave enough cover to a robber waiting for his prey to come down the trail. I checked the map again. This was where they had robbed Dugan, I was pretty sure of that.

I climbed the peaks again, but I really wasn't looking for tracks or shells this time. There would at least be tracks—I was sure of that and found them at two of the three peaks. I was more interested in whether there was enough cover near those two peaks to turn the tables and get the drop on the robbers.

After scouting around for a half hour, I was convinced we could draw them out. If there was somebody brave enough to ride that trail down there and draw out the highwaymen, I was convinced that a few well-placed riflemen up here could turn the tables on them and end their bushwhacking days.

A glance overhead told me the day was more than half gone. I returned to the trail and made my decision to return home. It would be worth looking at some point for a place where they might have stored some of the stolen ore, but I would have to look for it later.

NINE
LEAVING TOWN

Joanna moved toward the doctor's office. She had closed the bakery early so she could go visit Sarge at a more reasonable hour. By the time she was usually done cleaning up, Sarge was likely to be asleep. She gathered up her skirts and kept an eye out for the mud puddles in the street. On her way to the boardwalk, a voice from a doorway caught her by surprise.

"Psst!" She scanned the street. "Over here by the doorway, ma'am!"

It took her a moment to locate him. Now, she saw the bully who had fought Lat in the street outside the bakery several days ago. She stared, trying to remember his name. Otis, she thought, that was his name.

He stepped away from the door to the feed store, holding his hat in both hands now and looking warily up and down the street. He turned to face Joanna, still speaking in a loud whisper.

"I'd be plumb obliged to talk to you, ma'am, but it wouldn't do me no good at all to be seen out there on Main Street with you." He stayed where he was, shifting from one foot to the other, looking up and down the street.

Joanna debated with herself for just a moment, then walked over, stepped up to the boardwalk, and stopped a foot or two short of him. "Otis, right? You fought with Latigo Smith outside the bakery," she said.

He nodded, touching his jaw and frowning. "He done tore down my meathouse," he mumbled. Joanna waited for him to tell her what this was about.

"I want to talk to Sarge over there to the doc's office," he said softly. "But I don't want to disturb him none or make him worry none. I aim to talk to him peaceful-like, if'n he'll talk to me."

Joanna stared at him, trying to decide whether she believed him. Otis stood and waited, passing his hat back and forth nervously between his hands. He seemed like he was being truthful, but it really wasn't her decision. It would be up to Sarge. She told Otis it would be Sarge's decision.

Otis nodded and stayed where he was, saying nothing. Finally, he shrugged. "Kin I jest walk in there an' talk to him, do ya think?"

Joanna shook her head and stepped away. "Wait here," she told him. "I'll ask Sarge. If it's okay with him, I'll tell you when I come out."

Otis nodded and stepped back against the wall of the feed store. Joanna continued down to the doctor's office. Sarge was alone in the room when she came in.

He started to sit up in his bed, but she moved over and told him to lie back down.

Joanna pulled a chair up next to the bed and took a seat. She studied his face. "I'm glad you've stayed here at the doctor's office," she said. "How are you feeling?"

Sarge passed a hand over his ribs and grimaced. "It ain't too bad," he allowed. "Them ribs hurt the most, and the doc, he's givin' me mostly soup and scrambled eggs and such cause my jaw hurts, but I'm about ready to tie into a steak or somethin'." He glanced at her sideways. "I'm about ready to bust right outta here," he added, looking toward the door. "I ain't sure how long it's gonna be safe for me to be jest lyin' around in here."

He had a point there, she had to agree. "Preacher's acting as the sheriff these last couple days," she told him. "That mayor, Knowles, he just lets Preacher do whatever he wants. He's got a couple new gunhands just helping themselves to the cash in the stores. I expect the bakery will get robbed next."

Sarge nodded grimly. "What about Latigo?" he mumbled, rubbing his sore jaw. "He ain't gonna take this stuff layin' down. What's he gonna do?"

Joanna stared at him, looking at the bruises on his face and the stiff way he'd laid back on the bed. He wasn't well enough to leave here, but if he stayed, they might just finish him off in here.

She leaned forward to whisper. "Lat has been talking to a miner named Dugan. Big man, long red hair and beard."

Sarge nodded instantly. "Spends a lot of time at the

Suds 'n Such," he said. "Never had no trouble with him. Good thing, too. That feller could pack a big punch if he wanted to. Wouldn't never want to rile him up."

"Well," Joanna said, "Ike Penfield or Preacher Dalton, or both of them, have him riled up now. Their gang robbed him on the trail from Ice Lake, trying to bring his ore to town and sell it. He's going to talk to the other miners. Lat wants to take the fight to Penfield's gang."

Sarge grinned and punched the bed with this fist. "I knowed it!" he crowed. He threw back the bedcovers. "I got to git me out there to Lat's ranch."

Joanna put out a hand to stop him. "Better wait until it's dark," she advised. "I'll make sure they saddle your horse down at the livery. Right now, though, there's a guy that wants to talk to you. Says he wants no trouble. I think I believe him."

"Who?" was all Sarge said.

"That guy named Otis. The one that fought with Lat out in front of the bakery. He's out there waiting. I told him I'd ask you if you'll talk with him."

"Huh," Sarge said thoughtfully. He reached under the pillow and pulled out his Colt, sliding it under the covers and holding it with his right hand. "I'll give him a chance, but I don't trust none of that bunch too much." He leaned back and arranged his pillow with his left hand. "He kin come in," he told her.

Joanna closed the office door softly behind her and moved over to Otis, who was still standing in the shadow of the feed store. She nodded her head at the doctor's office. "You can go in," she said. She took a step away and turned back. "If you go in peaceful," she added, "then you can go talk to him."

Otis waited in the long early evening shadows and watched the street for several minutes after the bakery lady had moved on. Finally, he crossed quickly and let himself into the doctor's office. Sarge was propped up against several pillows. Only his left hand was above the sheets.

Otis stepped warily into the room, watching Sarge's right arm, which was mostly under the covers. "I reckon you've got ahold of that hogleg, down there under them covers," Otis murmured. "I ain't come to cause trouble, but you kin keep ahold of it if you want to. Jest listen to what I got to say. I won't come no closer." He spread his jacket open. "I ain't got no gun on me."

Sarge relaxed slightly, still watching Otis like a hawk watches a prairie dog. "Say what you got to say," he growled.

"Preacher's boys are comin' for you in here," Otis blurted. "Mebbe not tonight, but pretty soon." He paused, watching Sarge's face. "They're comin' after yore friend Holt, too, down there to the Suds 'n Such. They're gonna stage another fight, but this time, my old partner Bert is gonna gun Holt down. Penfield or Preacher, one of 'em, is gonna take that saloon for themselves. Penfield thinks he's gonna take it, but I ain't so sure it won't be Preacher. I don't trust neither of 'em no more."

Sarge stayed quiet for a while, studying Otis's face and deciding which question he wanted to ask first.

"Why don't you trust 'em no more?" he asked suspiciously.

"They done promised me fiddy dollars if I started a dust-up with that Lat Smith guy. They promised Bert the same to take you down. They didn't pay no money when Smith taken me down. They didn't pay Bert neither."

Sarge still said nothing. Otis studied him from across the room. "Then they sent those two boys to jump you down at the Suds 'n Such. They done set up an ambush, since they was afraid you'd get 'em in a stand-up fight."

"Why would you help me?" Sarge demanded. "You'd be helpin' Lat Smith, and he done busted you up the other day."

"Yeah, he settled my hash pretty good," Otis admitted. He watched Sarge's face. "He done it fair 'n square, though. Didn't throw no cheap punches or nuthin'. I expect I could trust him a lot better than Preacher."

"You said Bert ain't yore partner no more," Sarge observed. "Is he still in with Preacher Dalton and them?"

"Yep, he is," Otis nodded. "He wants their money bad. If he gets him a good payday, he'll be gone, but him an' me ain't gonna ride together no more. I ain't proud of what I've done since I met Bert."

"Why should I trust you?" Sarge asked.

"You must know what a chance I taken jest comin' in here to talk to you," Otis growled. "I'm a dead man if'n they know I tole you this."

Sarge studied Otis's face a while longer and decided. "Don't know why I believe you, but I do," he sighed. He grabbed a piece of paper and pencil off the table next to him and scribbled a note, stopping once in a while to stare at the ceiling. Finally, he folded up the note.

"Kin you read?" he asked Otis.

Otis shook his head.

"Didn't think so," Sarge mumbled. He held out the note. "Do you know that kid that works in the saloon kitchen, doin' dishes and stuff?"

Otis nodded.

"Give this here note to that kid, an' tell him he has to show it to Holt at the saloon and Joanna, the bakery lady."

Otis took the note and stuffed it in his pocket. "I gotta git outta town after this," Otis told him. "Kin you help me?"

Sarge sighed and leaned back. His right hand appeared above the sheets for the first time. "Be at the livery stable a couple hours after it gets dark tonight," he answered. "You can ride with us. I'll tell you where we're goin' later."

Otis put his hat on, looked both ways before stepping out the door, then hustled across Main Street.

━━━

Joanna turned up the lantern and moved it to the kitchen, waving at Herbie, Holt's saloon helper, to come with her. She pulled out a chair, smoothed out the note, and read it slowly.

When she looked up, Herbie was watching her closely. "Did you read this?" she asked.

Herbie shook his head back and forth. Joanna watched him closely until he hung his head and nodded slowly. "I read a little bit," he said.

Joanna folded up the note and leaned in. "You know you can't tell anybody, don't you, Herbie?"

He nodded vigorously. "Yes, ma'am. I won't tell nobody, I promise."

"Good, Herbie." She patted his hand. "Now you have to get back to the saloon and get back to work like always, before anybody notices you're gone." Herbie nodded and dashed out the door.

She read the note one more time:

Holt and Joanna,

> *We got to git outta town right now. Meet me at the livry stabl in about two or three hours. Don't tell nobody. Otis mite come to. We got to trust him,*
> > *I think.*

Sarge

Joanna sighed, then picked up a bag and stuffed some bread into it. She looked around and left by the back door, making sure she had things locked up. Not that it would make any difference, she knew that. They would break in here and take what they wanted.

Circling around to her room at the boarding house, she grabbed a canvas bag and tucked in her coat and one change of clothes. She left by the back door and took the alley down to the livery stable. A voice startled her when she stepped inside.

Holt came forward out of the shadows. "We've got horses saddled up, and Sarge and Otis are holding them out there in the trees. We've got to go to Lat's ranch. Maybe to the hideout. We'll have to look things over when we get there."

Joanna nodded and followed Holt out the back of the livery stable. She could see the men and horses as they approached a clump of trees. She reached out to help Sarge mount, but he brushed her hand away, mounting with a small moaning sound.

Holt led the way down the trail toward Lat's ranch. Joanna wondered if she would ever see her bakery again.

Dugan pushed through the batwing doors at the Suds 'n Such and took his usual seat at a table by the window. The server girl came along with a shot of his whiskey, but Dugan waved it aside. The girl's mouth opened in astonishment.

"Beer," Dugan growled. He patted his stomach. "Et too much over at the café." The girl smiled and brought his beer.

He sipped the beer and made a face. He liked his whiskey better, but he had to keep a clear head tonight. He was looking for a few miners to give him the news Latigo Smith was looking for.

A couple more pulls at the beer and Dugan was

feeling better about things. Right up until he saw the guy with the yellow hair and the guys walking behind him into the saloon. Dugan had never seen this guy in the saloon before, but Dugan knew exactly where he *HAD* seen him—on the Ice Lake Basin Trail. This was the guy who'd stepped out from the brush and started the holdup.

Two guys trailed along behind the guy with the yellow hair. One of them called the holdup man Deuce. Dugan hadn't seen the other two, but he was willing to bet they'd both been on the other end of a Winchester, up behind the rocks while Deuce was taking his money. Dugan pulled his collar up and yanked down his hat to hide his red hair.

When the girl came with another beer, Dugan took it and sailed a coin across the table. She scooped it up in one motion and left. Dugan glanced sideways as Deuce and his two guys sat at the table next to him. They started on whiskey, and it was going down their throats in a hurry. Dugan moved to face away from them, then inched his chair closer to their table. That whiskey would loosen their tongues and get them talking a lot louder in no time. Dugan knew that from personal experience.

When the girl brought his fifth beer, Dugan slugged it down in one long gulp and stared at the table in front of him. He hadn't heard more than a few words now and then, but he'd heard enough. The words *move some ore* and *Ice Lake* were plain enough. He hadn't heard when they'd planned on it, but Lat Smith would want to move on this. This was better than news about guys who'd been robbed a few weeks back. This gang was moving ore down the Ice Lake Basin Trail, probably from a hiding place near the lake at the other end of the trail.

"Beer? You ain't drinkin' nuthin' but beer these days?"

Dugan looked up to see the grinning face of a miner he'd seen around here from time to time. Barnes worked along the Hardrock Hundred Trail, Dugan knew that. He also knew that Barnes and two of his partners had been robbed, probably by these same guys—Deuce and his buddies, no doubt.

Dugan waved off the server as she approached to take Barnes's order. He leaned across the table. "You and your partners got robbed a couple weeks back, right?"

Barnes stared across the table and nodded. "Yep. You know something about that?"

Dugan lowered his voice. "You want a chance to git yore money back?"

Barnes nodded slowly. Dugan stood. "Foller me," he muttered.

Preacher leaned back at his table in the café and stared at the kid across the table from him. The kid couldn't be over twenty years old, but he'd swaggered across the place like he owned it and plopped himself down in the chair across from Preacher.

"Penfield wants to know when he can move up here from Leadville," the kid announced. "Wants to know when you're gonna wrap things up around here. It's gotta be soon," he finished importantly.

The kid looked around, spotted the waitress, and started to raise his hand. Preacher reached across the table, twisted the kid's wrist, and pinned it to the table. The kid's eyes widened. He opened his mouth to holler, then thought better of it.

"You take the train back yonder to where you come. Do that first thing tomorrow," Preacher hissed. "Tell Penfield he can come down any time."

The kid left with his tail between his legs as soon as Preacher let go of his wrist. Preacher leaned back and stared across the street at the Suds 'n Such. By the day after tomorrow, he planned to make the back room over there his office. Penfield wanted it, but Preacher had other plans. He studied the menu and ordered some food.

Twenty minutes later, Bert, the gunhand, came in and walked to the table. Preacher pointed at the empty chair. Bert took a seat.

Preacher took a bite of his stew and reached for his coffee. "We don't make no moves tonight," he told Bert. "Tomorrow night. We take down Holt at the saloon. Take Blondie or Otis with you. Talk to a couple of them gunhands Penfield sent down here yesterday. Tell 'em to earn their money over at the doc's office. Take out that Sarge guy in his sick bed over there. If anybody gives you any trouble, take care of them, too."

Bert nodded and stood. "Hey!" Preacher's voice stopped him in his tracks. "Look out for that giant redheaded miner. He's trouble."

Bert nodded again and left. He decided he would take Blondie with him to the saloon. He couldn't trust Otis anymore. And he expected a good payday for this. He would get paid twice. Preacher didn't know that Penfield had paid Bert to watch Preacher. He wondered how long it would be before one of them paid him to kill the other one. He was pretty sure that was coming.

TEN
BOYD AND BOYD

B ert went directly to the saloon, not because Preacher had given him orders, but because he really needed a drink. He shoved aside a drunken miner on his way through the doors and proceeded directly to the bar.

The old guy in suspenders served him the whiskey, that wasn't too unusual. Holt was probably in the back. Bert turned and rested his elbows on the bar while he downed the first whiskey. There were a bunch of drunken miners in here, just like most nights, but nobody bothered Bert. Maybe it had to do with those guns hanging from his hips.

A grin creased his mouth while he turned back to survey the room again, holding his second whiskey. There would be a lot more respect for him soon. After tomorrow night, after he'd cut down that Holt guy, hiding behind his little shotgun. Folks around here would really cut a wide swath around him.

The third whiskey was working hard to deaden his

brain when he noticed something that made him frown. There were a couple guys at a table over there he recognized. Not the big redheaded miner, he was buried in his beer at the next table over. He was minding his own business. Bert frowned again, but this time, it was because he was concentrating, and tonight it was harder than usual. The whiskey was working on him, but he thought he'd seen at least one of those guys before.

Bert wasn't thinking any better after the fourth whiskey, but after the three guys at the table got up and walked out, he remembered where he'd seen one of them. He was one of Penfield's guys—one of the guys robbing the miners on their way into town. He'd been in Penfield's office with Preacher one time, and Bert had met that guy. Bert stared at his boots and tried to figure out why Penfield's highwaymen would be here in Silverton. Penfield was down there in Leadville, wasn't he?

Penfield had some dangerous men there in Leadville, Bert had to admit that. There was a couple of 'em he wouldn't want to call out. The twins, what was their name? Boyd, that was it. They had first names, but Bert didn't know them. Dangerous with a rifle or a pistol, that's what the word was on those twins. Nobody would brace either of 'em. Well, maybe Preacher would.

Motion in the room caught his eye before he solved the puzzle about why Penfield's robbers were here in town. The big redhead was leaving, along with somebody else who was clearly another miner, judging by his clothes. You could always tell. Bert's upper lip curled in disgust. All day long, swinging a pickaxe or swirling a pan around in freezing water, and what did they have to show for it? Nothing, after they got relieved of their gold on the way to town. Fools, all of 'em. Penfield's boys were about to clean 'em out again.

The room was swimming around a little after the fifth whiskey. Maybe it was swimming around a lot. Bert decided to call it a night. Nothing was happening around here, anyway. It was after he'd fallen face down on his cot at the boarding house that a thought finally made its way through his brain. He hadn't seen Holt at the Suds 'n Such tonight. Not all night long.

The last thought Bert had before settling into a deep, steady snore was that Holt should have been there. Bert was sure he'd seen Holt in there every time he had gone to the saloon. Preacher would want to know about it. Maybe he shouldn't bring it up, though. Preacher was a dangerous man, and he could get downright grumpy.

By the time his throbbing headache eased up the next morning, Bert decided for sure it was best not to tell Preacher he hadn't seen Holt at the saloon. No sense in getting Preacher all riled up.

I'm a light sleeper by nature, and it has saved my hide a time or two. The thing is, I was getting used to that big feather bed left behind by Jed and his family at the ranch house. Maybe that was why I didn't hear the horses coming into the yard and didn't hear anybody dismounting or moving toward the house. Probably a couple of the horses neighed, and I didn't hear that, either.

It was the big *hello the house* somebody yelled that got me sitting straight up and reaching for my gun belt, hanging on the bedpost next to my head. Then, I stopped reaching for the guns. I knew Holt's voice, even when it brought me out of a dead man's sleep.

I clambered out of the bed and headed for the front door, then thought better of it and went back for my pants. Didn't nobody want to see me in my long johns, I was sure of that.

When I opened the front door, nobody I saw there surprised me too much, except for Otis. I stared at him hard as he trooped in with the others. He raised both hands in the air.

"You whupped me fair and square, knuckle and skull," he declared. "You can ask Sarge over there why I'm here. He told me to come. You boys are straight shooters and them other ones ain't. Besides that, I don't want to git into it with 'ol Dugan."

I chuckled and stood aside to let him in. To my surprise, Joanna was there, too. I was glad to see her, but I knew she wouldn't have come if things hadn't gone bad back there in Silverton. She loved that bakery. She pulled my head down and gave me a kiss, then went to light a lantern and set it on the table.

Sarge walked by and took a seat with a little groan. I glanced over at Joanna and she just shrugged. "We all had to come. Sarge, too. You need to hear what Dugan told us," she said. "None of us could stay in town after tonight."

Dugan pulled something from inside his shirt and

spread it out on the table with his big, meaty paws. "Made me a better map of the Ice Lake Basin Trail," he explained. He looked over at me. "Heard somethin' at the saloon tonight, Cap'n," he said. "I think them boys is getting' ready to move some stolen ore from where they've got it hid. Just like you thought, Cap'n. Maybe we can take it back."

I was looking at one guy standing around the table that I didn't know. Dugan followed where I was looking and pointed at the new guy. "That there is Barnes," he explained. "He got robbed by the same bunch over on the Hardrock Hundred Trail a couple weeks ago. He wants his money back, jest like the rest of us."

Dugan went on to tell me he'd sat at a table next to a guy at the Suds 'n Such who had been the one who'd stepped out to hold him up in the trail to town. "Sure as I'm standing here, Cap'n, that was him. He didn't look my way, so I just set there and listened in. He said *Ice Lake* a couple times an' he said somethin' about moving ore down the trail. Didn't say when, but I don't think they're gonna have no grass growin' under their feet. They probly git paid when they take the ore to town."

Everybody seemed to be watching me. "Well, maybe this is our best chance. I went out there and scouted the trail," I told them. "The best spot to take 'em out would be right where they held up Dugan. I don't guess they'd be expecting somebody to do the same to them."

I tapped a finger on the table and thought things over. "They must be hiding the ore up at the end of the trail, by the lake somewhere. Maybe we can find the main stash later."

I looked over at Dugan and Barnes. "How many?" I asked. "How many guys do you think are in that gang?"

They looked at each other, then Dugan spoke for both of them. "Five, I think. Maybe only four, but I think five."

I looked around the room, trying to figure out how many guns we could bring to the fight. I knew I could count on Holt and Dugan. I wasn't sure about the rest.

"Me," barked Otis. "I ain't just good with my fists. I can hit what I'm aimin' at with a rifle."

"Me," said Barnes. "I can use a rifle too, and I'll do what it takes to get the money back for me and my friends."

Sarge fought his way out of his chair. "You can't leave me behind, Pilgrim. My old ribs hurt a little, but I can sit my horse and sight my Winchester. You'd better be countin' on me."

Joanna stepped forward and linked her arm through mine. "And me," she said. "You know I can shoot, and you're not leaving me behind, either."

I looked around the room and grinned. "I guess we're all gonna go. We've got seven guns to their five and we'll get the drop on 'em. Everybody gets some sleep and packs a little food. We'll leave at first light and stake out our position up on the trail."

Ike Penfield was just finishing his lunch in the new gambling club he had built in Leadville. He made more money in his other clubs because he could fleece the miners and the occasional drifter or cowboy in those clubs. This one, though, was by invitation only. Penfield didn't have to rub elbows with the ordinary people in here. Plus, he had hired the best cook he could find in this town to prepare his meals.

He could see the kid he had sent up to Silverton a few days ago to get a report from Preacher. The kid had been sitting across the private café for about a half hour now, just squirming in his chair and waiting for Penfield to call him over.

Penfield took his time finishing dessert and coffee while he looked at a few papers he'd brought with him for lunch. He knew he could have just sent a telegram to Preacher, but he liked to have his message delivered in person when he wanted to intimidate. He stared sourly out the side window. Preacher Dalton was hard to intimidate. There could be some trouble brewing there.

Finally, Penfield pushed his dishes aside and waved for the kid to come over. The kid waited while a waiter cleared the dishes away, then stood nervously while Penfield lit a cigar and blew a few puffs.

"Well?" Penfield growled.

"Preacher says you can come down any time," the kid blurted. "Silverton is all ready for you, sir."

"Hmmmph." Penfield squinted through the smoke, surprised but happy to hear the news. He had to admit it, the Preacher got things done. He fished in his vest pocket, then flipped a coin to the kid, who caught it expertly.

"And tell the manager to stake you to ten dollars at the poker table," Penfield said, feeling generous at the good news. Plus, he knew the kid would lose the ten dollars and more at the table.

"Thank you, sir!" The kid did everything but salute, then bolted away.

Penfield stayed where he was, puffing on his cigar and thinking about the Preacher situation. He might need an ace in the hole to deal with Preacher before it was all done. He stubbed out his cigar and went to find the club manager.

The manager stood up behind his desk when he saw Penfield coming. "Have either of the Boyd twins been in today?" he asked.

The club manager shook his head. "Not yet, sir, but they're in here most days. They'll probably be in here in another few hours."

Penfield nodded. "Send them over to my office when you see them."

He toured all his saloons before returning to his office. He had to be sure things were running like they should before moving his operations to Silverton. There would be more money to be made in Silverton, he was sure of that.

A brawl in the street got his attention on the way back to his office. He noticed money changing hands after the fight. He needed to look into that. He could stage some fights, rig the outcomes, and make more money.

Penfield had dug out a bottle of brandy to celebrate

his move to Silverton and had lowered the contents by a few inches when the Boyd brothers tapped on the door and let themselves in.

Penfield didn't know where these two had learned to handle a gun the way they had, but he didn't care. He'd hired them away from a railroad security job and used their skills several times. These guys were still hungry. Ruthless, too. They hadn't made a lot of money so far, and they needed Penfield to fatten their bankrolls.

Penfield cut right to the point. "I'll be movin' up to Silverton," he announced. "I need you boys to run things here while I'm gone." He looked at them sharply. "I'm gonna increase what I pay you, but I want just as much money coming to me. Understood?"

They nodded in unison, which was an annoying habit they had. They turned to go.

"One more thing," Penfield growled. They turned. "I might have a, uh...problem with Preacher Dalton. If I do, I'm gonna send a telegram, and I want one of you to come down and take care of things. I don't care which one of you comes down. The other one will stay here to keep things running smoothly."

They nodded in unison again. Penfield waved them out the door and returned to his brandy bottle. He'd been planning to take the train down tomorrow, but it wouldn't hurt, he decided, to wait for an extra day or two. He had a few other things to finish up around here.

Preacher listened to Bert's account of activities in the Suds 'n Such Saloon from the night before. He locked in on Bert with an unblinking stare. Not that he wondered if Bert was lying about last night—he was sure about that. He was just having trouble deciding which part of the story was a lie.

The interesting part about the story was the part about Penfield's guys in the saloon. Preacher hadn't known they were down here, but he was sure Bert was right about these guys. The name Deuce was familiar, and what Bert said fit the description of the guy Penfield used for holdups on the trails. The idea they were moving some of their ill-gotten gains sounded like there might be a little cash up for grabs.

Preacher didn't pay much attention to the part about the huge redheaded miner hanging around the place. He had caused no trouble last night. He was probably too drunk to be a problem. Preacher was still thinking about whether he could make a move on that ore they were moving.

It was that last part—the part about Holt having been in the saloon all night long that brought his attention back. Bert started to crawfish around in his chair. Bert couldn't seem to look Preacher in the eye. A little trickle of sweat started down his cheek and disappeared into his beard. That, Preacher decided, was the part Bert was lying about.

If Holt wasn't there, where had he gone? Preacher decided it was time to check a few things out for himself. He would deal with Bert later. He waved Bert out of his room at the boarding house, strapped on his guns, and stepped outside.

The first stop was going to be the doctor's office. He had a sinking feeling already that the old coot from the saloon wasn't here anymore. Maybe he'd underestimated how tough that old man was.

When he threw open the door to the doctor's office and stormed into the back room, the bed was empty. Old Doc Adams was pulling bottles out of a cabinet and stuffing them into his medical bag, grumbling to himself.

Preacher pointed at the empty bed. "Where did he go?" Preacher demanded.

Doc Adams snorted and shook his head. "Danged if I know. He don't consult with me about nuthin'." He snapped his bag shut and shoved past Preacher. "All I know is he was here yesterday, just as cussed and ornery as ever, and this mornin', he was gone. That's just all I know." The door slammed loudly behind him.

Preacher stood outside the doctor's office, staring up and down the street. It was too early for the saloon to be open. On a hunch, he walked down to the bakery. It was locked. He hammered on the door and got no answer. Walking around to the back, he forced his way in through the back door. The place was empty. It should have been booming at this hour of the morning. Preacher cursed under his breath as he let himself out the front door.

He was there as soon as the saloon opened. Preacher was already beginning to see some good news about what had happened today. Penfield would be furious, but Preacher was tired of keeping Penfield happy. Besides, Penfield would have plenty of other stuff to worry about if his gold ore shipment got robbed. Preacher had a feeling that was about to happen. Why else would all these people leave town?

The old guy in suspenders who worked the bar looked at him blankly when Preacher demanded to see Holt.

"Ain't seen him, neither last night nor today. It ain't like him. He's always here, but today he ain't." The old man said nothing else. He stopped talking and stared at Preacher nervously.

Preacher walked through the saloon and opened the door to the back room. Holt had an office set up back here. Preacher sat down in the desk chair and looked around. This place, he decided, would be his. If Penfield wanted it, he'd better have the guns to back it up. It was time to change the deal with Penfield. Preacher got up and walked back to the bar area to give himself a free whiskey.

ELEVEN
PENFIELD AND PREACHER

P acking the ore and nuggets out of the abandoned mine at Ice Lake had turned out to be tougher than Deuce had expected. There were two reasons for that. One, Deuce hadn't packed any of it out of there himself. He just gave orders and drank whiskey while his boys did that. And two, they were taking a larger shipment this time than they had before.

Penfield had told him to take one more pack mule this time, so Deuce had a pretty good idea how much Penfield wanted brought down, but Deuce was feeling underpaid for the risks he had taken with this operation.

They had used two pack mules last time, but this time, they had four. After all, Deuce reasoned, he had four men, including his sister's kid, who had begged to come along with him. Four men could lead four pack mules, plus they could load a little extra in the saddlebags on their horses. That added up to a lot more money for Deuce. Penfield didn't need to know about that.

They had hidden the ore deep inside an abandoned mine. Those were Penfield's orders, and for once, Deuce agreed with Penfield. They didn't need some lucky miner wandering in there and taking the loot. It was deep inside the old mine, around two bends in the trail and stashed up against an icy wall.

The darkness inside was something else to deal with. Each man carried a lantern inside. They set the lanterns down every fifty feet or so, which gave them enough light to see on their way in and out. Still, it took a handheld lantern or two at the back to find the ore and load it into burlap bags to carry out.

There was another problem, too. The path going in and out was icy. They hadn't gone clear up to the lake, which was even higher up, but it was around ten thousand feet where the abandoned mine lay. No sun got inside, of course, and the path was always wet, somehow. Deuce had taken a bad fall twice. No amount of cursing seemed to help.

It had taken two days, but Deuce was about ready to call it quits. Starting at sunup each day, he had lost track of the number of trips they had taken, loading heavy bags onto their backs and working carefully out along that icy path. A couple of 'em had tried loading the ore into crates and carrying the ore out in pairs on each end of the crate. That had turned out to be harder than carrying a bag on their backs.

Deuce called a halt to it at the end of the second day. They loaded up the pack mules and put a little more in each saddlebag. One look at the eyes staring back at him, and Deuce knew he would have to promise more money for this. He would give them the full thirty apiece. He had an extra pack mule to keep for himself, and nobody the wiser.

Besides, he would only give ten or fifteen to his sister's kid, Pierce. The kid was lucky to come along on this, and he hadn't really done his share, in Deuce's opinion. Sixteen was old enough to do a full day's work as a man. The kid would have to toughen up.

A look at the sky told Deuce they had about two hours to work their way down the trail. If they could get down maybe fifteen hundred feet lower, camp would be a lot warmer tonight.

Deuce had made one other change on this trip, and the boys were all in agreement on this one. He'd used a scout on the other trip, a guy who'd ridden ahead and checked out the places where somebody could hide under cover and rob them. Deuce and his boys knew all the places—after all, they'd used them to get this ore. Now, he needed everybody to lead those pack mules. These miners didn't have the firepower to rob his boys. Besides that, the miners just flat out weren't salty enough to pull off a robbery, in Deuce's opinion.

Deuce gave the order to move out. He couldn't wait to break into his whiskey bottle after they had a little fire going to cook their dinner at the camp.

Penfield decided two days was long enough to postpone his move up to Silverton. He had drilled the Boyd brothers on running things here in Leadville, and he'd made it clear he expected somebody on the train every two weeks to bring him his cash. Penfield made a mental note to visit the bank in Silverton early on. He expected to be treated like royalty there.

The narrow-gauge rail was a new thing to Penfield, and the country they passed through on the trip caught him by surprise. Not many things surprised Penfield anymore, but he had some idea how tough it must have been to lay the rails for this four-hour trip.

The train wound through tall stands of aspen trees, with the Rocky Mountains framed in the background. Penfield noticed they crossed the Animas River at several points, with each crossing requiring a bridge. The railroad was just a way to get the gold and silver out of Silverton, and Penfield grinned to himself when he thought about that. He would ship out a lot of that gold and silver after Deuce Thorne and his boys did their work.

Silverton came into view and Penfield reached out to shake his assistant awake. He'd brought only one clerk with him, only because he couldn't be bothered to do banking work or arrange ore shipments. When the train ground to a stop, the two of them were the first ones off the train.

Penfield handed his bags to his clerk with instructions to find the best room in the best hotel in town. That was for Penfield, of course. The clerk would have to make do with whatever he could afford on the tiny amount of money Penfield paid him.

Penfield walked a few blocks until he came to what looked like the center of business in the town. He stepped over to inspect a name scratched on the street sign. "Greene Street," he muttered to himself. Scanning in all directions, his eyes stopped on a saloon sign two blocks down. Moving in that direction, he could soon make out the name on the sign, *Suds 'n Such*.

He stopped to pull a watch from his vest pocket. It was three o'clock in the afternoon. Penfield wanted a beer and he wanted to find Preacher, in that order. With a little luck, he could find both at the same place.

Penfield pushed through the saloon doors and moved toward the bar. The crowd at this hour was better than he expected. That was a good sign for him, since he intended to own this saloon soon.

He stepped up to a long, rough-hewn plank running along most of one wall and stared at the old guy in suspenders filling orders behind the bar. "Beer," he barked, plunking a coin down on the wood surface.

The old bartender put his beer on the bar and scooped up the coin with one easy motion. Penfield put a hand on his wrist to stop the old man from moving away. "I need to talk to Holt, the owner of this place," he muttered.

The old man looked in both directions, then glanced over toward a closed door behind the bar. "Holt don't own this place no more," he said, almost under his breath. "I ain't seen Holt in a few days now."

Penfield stopped with the beer halfway to his mouth. "He doesn't own it anymore? What do you mean? Who owns it?"

The old man stared down at his wrist, which

Penfield still had pinned to the bar. He cleared his throat and stared behind Penfield, fear in his eyes.

Penfield looked behind him and saw a gunfighter he'd hired a few months back to keep the cash flowing in Leadville. He searched his brain for the man's name. Bert somebody, that was it. The man met his eyes, nodded slightly, then looked away.

Penfield let go of the old man's wrist and repeated his question in a softer tone. "Who owns the saloon now?" he asked.

The old man swallowed twice and looked Penfield in the eyes for the first time. "Guy by the name of Preacher Dalton is my boss now," he said, looking again at Bert as he did so. "Preacher Dalton," he repeated.

Ike Penfield felt anger and worry flare up inside him at the same time. Preacher was clearly moving in on a saloon he'd wanted for himself. At the same time, he was a little afraid of a showdown with Preacher. He'd certainly hoped to put it off, at the least, until things were running smoothly here in Silverton.

Penfield nodded, his eyes darting toward the closed door the old man had looked at earlier. "Is Preacher Dalton here right now?" he asked. His question came out in a low hiss. The old man backed off two steps.

"He's here," the bartender quavered.

Penfield picked up his beer and looked around for the nearest empty table. "I'll be over there at that table," he said, pointing. "Could you tell Preacher Dalton that Ike Penfield is here and wants to talk to him?"

The old man headed for the closed door at a shambling trot. Penfield moved toward the empty table, casting a quick glance at Bert, who nodded and looked away. Penfield made a mental note to find out where Bert's loyalties lay right now.

A door slammed in the back and Penfield looked up to see Preacher Dalton coming around the corner of the bar, battered black hat in place as always. Funny, Penfield thought, he didn't remember Dalton being this big and thickly built. Penfield thought about his pistol, packed away in his luggage. Maybe it was better that he didn't have it on him.

Preacher yanked out the chair across the table from Penfield, flipped it around, and straddled it with his arms hanging over the back of the chair. Penfield didn't miss the fact that Preacher's eyes swept down to look for a gun belt. Penfield plastered a small grin on his face. A little voice in the back of his head told him to go easy.

"The old codger at the bar told me Holt isn't in town anymore," Penfield said smoothly. "Looks like you've made some good progress around this town."

"Yup." Preacher fished a cigar out of his pocket, lit it, and blew the smoke at Penfield. "We've pretty near run ever'body outta town that could cause any trouble. Ain't seen Holt or that Latigo Smith guy for a couple days." He took a couple more puffs and stared at Penfield through narrowed eyes. "That sheriff was no dang use. He's left town too. Was he kin to you?"

Penfield shifted uncomfortably and shook his head. "Nope. He was kin to Bowles, the mayor." He left out the fact that he was related to Bowles. Penfield paused, thinking of a way to get back in control of this pow-wow.

Preacher jumped in again, leaning forward on the table. "I done taken over this here bar. It's gonna be my office. Where I run things, give my orders and such." His stare into Penfield's eyes was a challenge.

Penfield blinked and finally nodded. "Nice saloon. Where do you have an office for me? What's around here for the taking that will bring some good money?"

Preacher stared for a while and threw him a bone. "That land agent of your'n didn't get nuthin' done. He's got him a good office across the street that might work pretty nice." He blew a couple more smoke rings. There's a gamblin' hall or two, and the bank might make you some money. I'm thinkin' I could get the banker to sign that over without no fuss."

That was better than Penfield had expected. It bought him some time to plan how to deal with Preacher, who had clearly stepped over the line. He held out his hand and stood. "Which way to the land office?"

Preacher pointed, and Penfield left. After stepping outside, he heard the doors open behind him and Bert, the gunfighter, stepped outside. He cleared his throat.

"You hired me, Mr. Penfield, an' I still work for you as far as I'm concerned. He spit into the street. That Preacher, he don't have no respect...don't treat people right."

Penfield said nothing. Bert walked away down the street. Penfield filed that away in his head. The guy could be useful at some point. Penfield saw the land office across the street and the Silverton Bank next to it. The bank wasn't much to look at, but Penfield could keep his money there and take the money that was in it already.

Stepping across the street, he shoved open the doors and stepped into the land office. Budge, the owner, looked up in irritation. Shock replaced the irritation when he recognized Penfield.

"I, uh, welcome, Mr. Penfield. I wasn't expecting you."

Penfield didn't answer. He walked around the office, looking out through the window and checking the furniture. "It's my office now," he announced.

Budge stared at him blankly.

"You didn't get me that ranch I wanted. Some guy named Latigo Smith bought it. You ain't done me much good around here. Get out."

Budge froze in his chair for a moment, then nodded slowly. "I have a little money in this drawer," he said. "Just let me get that money, and I'll move on."

Penfield moved around the desk, getting behind Budge, just in case there was a gun in the drawer. If there was, he intended to slam the drawer shut on Budge's fingers. "Okay," he growled slowly. "Nice and easy."

Budge eased the drawer open and pulled out a money belt. He left one hand on the desk while he pulled out the money belt with the other. He stepped around the desk and left the office without looking back. On his way to the train station, he got his things from the boarding house and put on the money belt under his shirt. Then he moved on down to the station and bought a ticket for the next train. He had seen what happened when these mining boomtowns got out of control.

Back in the land agent's office, which was now his office, Penfield took a seat behind the desk and watched Budge walk away. He could have kept the money, but he had a few more enemies than he'd like to have right now, so he'd let Budge walk. The few dollars in that money belt wouldn't matter.

Penfield allowed himself to feel some of the anger he'd squashed after Preacher had talked to him like that. The man had to be dealt with, which meant a telegram to Leadville to get one of the Boyd twins down here.

He stood and walked back out to Greene Street. This time, he was looking for the hotel. His clerk should have gotten him a room in there by now. After that, he would look for a saloon. Something other than the Suds 'n Such, he reminded himself with a growl under his breath.

Tomorrow, he decided, would be soon enough for a telegram to the Boyd twins. He would have to make sure the telegraph operator wasn't in Preacher's pocket. Penfield knew how to make sure the operator would stay quiet about his telegram. It wouldn't say that much anyway—it would just tell one of the twins to get down here in two or three days. Still, he didn't want Preacher to have that information.

Preacher strolled back into the office at the Suds 'n Such Saloon. That had gone better than he'd expected after he'd let Penfield know how things stood now. Still, he didn't think this was over. Penfield wasn't stupid enough to call out Preacher directly. He would send somebody else to do it.

Preacher pulled out a desk drawer and counted the cash they'd made at the saloon yesterday. He grinned and put it in the safe behind the desk. This was how things needed to be, with folks bringing the cash to him.

He returned to the desk chair and lit a fresh cigar while he thought about what Penfield might try to do to him. He would likely call down one of those twins, the gunfighters at Leadville. Preacher puffed a few times and thought that one over.

If just one of them came to town, Preacher would face him directly. He had seen those boys in a gunfight and they were good, but he was better. If there was just one of them, he would find an excuse to call him out and put him down.

If both of them came to town, well, that wasn't what he, Preacher, would call a fair fight. And Preacher knew what to do when it wasn't a fair fight. He knew how to even those odds. Accidents happened all the time, didn't they? Maybe Penfield needed to have an accident, too.

TWELVE
TURNING THE TABLES

We caught the Ice Lake Basin Trail at first light, cutting across the ranch and picking it up just a little west and north of Silverton. We moved along in total silence except for the occasional creak of saddle leather and snorts from the horses. I dismounted a couple times to see if I could pick up a recent trail of Penfield's outlaw gang moving to get the ore, but came away disappointed both times. Rains in the last few days seemed to have wiped out any hoofprints on the rocks and dust of the trail.

As the trail wound west and widened, the sun peaked over the mountain peaks. Joanna moved up to ride along beside me where the trail allowed it. The silence we'd kept up so far didn't seem as important now. There'd been no tracks left in the day and a half since we'd had rain, I was sure. They had a good head start on us, but that was okay. We needed to catch them on the way back. I glanced over at Joanna.

"I think we've got several hours' ride to get to the

canyon where that gang robbed Dugan," I told her. I glanced overhead. "We'll probably make it by the late afternoon. We can stake out our positions when we get there and make a small camp off the trail."

She reached over to pat my hand. "Sounds like a plan," she murmured, then fell back behind me on the path. I rode alone in front, trying to think of anything I'd overlooked. We were going up against a seasoned, salty bunch of thieves.

We had them outgunned, but just barely. I couldn't be sure how careful they would be on the way back. They might be pretty keen on getting all that ore cashed in, so that could make them a little careless. I had to admit I was counting on a little carelessness.

There were two other things we should have going for us. One, we should have surprise on our side. They had no reason to expect we'd be laying for them. Of course, that might depend on that carelessness thing. And two, I was determined we would have the high ground. We would have the same edge they'd had when they robbed the miners on this trail.

A few hours later, we crossed a rushing mountain stream, and I called a halt to water the horses. I noted with approval that most of the group pulled a biscuit or some jerky from their saddlebags and ate a little. I did the same, and we all drank and filled our waterskins. It was important to take care of things like food and water when there was time.

Dugan moved up beside me at the stream's edge, casting a critical eye at the trail ahead and the mountain peaks around us. "I think we're gettin' close," he murmured. "Mebbe another two hours' ride? Whaddya think?"

I nodded and moved to remount. "Yeah, I'd say right around two hours." I turned back to look at Holt and Sarge, who seemed to be holding up fine. The guy is made of shoe leather, I thought. I pointed at the trail. "If either of you boys spot some tracks I'm missin', sing out." They both nodded.

In another hour, I called a second halt and dismounted again to look at the trail. There were some faint tracks there. They were faint, and a little washed out. I was having trouble making any sense of them, but they looked like horse tracks. No wagons that I could see.

Sarge came up and kneeled beside me, studying the smudges in the dirt. He rose after a full minute, shaking his head. "Hard to tell much, boss," he said. "Lotta horses, maybe a few mules. Some of them strides look a little shorter and don't leave as much of a track, like they ain't being rode and don't got no weight on 'em right now. That's be mules, probly." He shook his head again. "Can't rightly tell how many of 'em are out there."

We pushed on for another hour. When the trail began a descent into a small valley with peaks jutting up on three sides, I knew we had reached the target area. I called a halt and waited for the others to join me. I looked at Dugan and he nodded his head.

"Yep," he growled, looking around with a sour expression. "This is it." He pointed up. "They was squirreled away up in them peaks."

Two hours later, we had our positions squared

away. There were two low peaks to the north of the trail and another to the south. That one was a little higher. I had Sarge and Otis on the closer peak to the north. Otis was plenty strong enough to give Sarge a hand if he needed it, and I had no doubt Sarge could hit whatever he wanted with that Winchester. Otis could lay down a little fire to help.

On the other peak to the north, I had Dugan and Barnes. I didn't know how accurate they were with the rifles, but between 'em, they could hold their own. I put Holt by himself on the lone peak to the south. I knew what he could do with a rifle. He had a good field of fire from his position.

I would be the one to step out on the trail and stop them when they came in range. Joanna would support from cover with the double-barreled shotgun. I told her to cock both barrels when they got close enough. That'll make any man stop and think whether he values his gold or his hide the most.

We pulled off the trail for a hundred yards and built a small campfire in a spot where the smoke could filter out through the aspen trees. There hadn't been any hostile Indian activity in this area for more than a year now, but we didn't need to stir any up with campfire smoke.

Joanna cooked a little venison stew over the campfire, and Sarge gave her a hand. My guess is you don't ride the trails and make as many camps as Sarge had without learning how to rustle up some vittles. Plus, he probably enjoyed Joanna's company. I couldn't blame him.

After the meal, we put out the campfire, and everybody went to their positions before bedding down. We had to be early risers—we couldn't take the chance they were close enough right now to get past us if they were moving at first light.

I shook out my bedroll on some pine needles, and Joanna did the same. She came to sit with me when I leaned back against a log, listening to the night sounds. "The tracks got clearer the closer we got to this place," she observed. "We're closing in, don't you think?"

"I do," I agreed. "Sarge and I took another look before dinner. Sarge thinks three, maybe four pack mules and another five horses. So," I said, "we're lookin' at five of those guys and they're haulin' an awful lot of ore and nuggets outta that stash they've got up that trail somewhere."

Joanna absorbed that information silently. Finally, in a voice that was no more than a whisper, she asked if I thought they were coming in the morning.

I shrugged in the darkness while I thought about my answer. "Good chance," I said finally. "The tracks they laid down at the start of the trail were old enough the rain had washed them out. The ones we can see around here are likely two or three days old. So, they had time..." My voice trailed away while I thought about it.

She snuggled up against me. "I'll have you covered," she whispered in the dark. "It's you and me, babe. It's our future here." She leaned over to give me a kiss.

After we'd gone to our bedrolls, I lay for a long time with my hands behind my head, staring up at the stars. That word, future, that had a pleasant sound to it. I needed to do something more about that future. I promised myself I would do that right after I got things settled down around this place.

———

Tyler Boyd scanned the telegram he'd just picked up on his daily visit to the telegraph office. As he read it, a grin creased his face. He folded the message one time, stuffed it into his pocket, and walked down to the office he now shared with his brother Harvey.

Harvey was settling into this job they had now, running Ike Penfield's gambling, saloon, and general shakedown business in Leadville. Harvey enjoyed giving those orders and nobody doubted he could back up those orders with his gun. Tyler, though, was getting pretty bored, and the brothers both knew Tyler was better with his six-gun. That made him ideal for these new orders from Penfield. He patted his pocket, making sure he had the telegram in there.

Harvey was barking at a couple of Penfield's enforcers when Tyler entered the office. He took a seat and waited while Harvey finished with the two men. They left with red faces and slammed the door on the way out. Tyler grinned at his brother.

"You're plumb enjoyin' this bossing around stuff," he crowed. Harvey chuckled and nodded, then his expression turned serious when Tyler pulled the telegram from his pocket. They'd both been expecting to hear something about Preacher Dalton.

Tyler smoothed out the message and shoved it

across the desk. "Looks like I need to take me a little trip up to Silverton," he said.

Harvey frowned and read the message:

LOOKS LIKE I NEED A LITTLE HELP WITH THE
PROBLEM WE TALKED ABOUT. STOP.
ONE OF YOU COME DOWN. STOP.
BE HERE THURSDAY. STOP.
PENFIELD

Harvey looked up at his brother. Today, he thought to himself, was Tuesday. That left just two days for one of them to get up to Silverton. Tyler, he could tell, was itching to go. That was a problem. Tyler was the faster of the two of them, but Harvey knew he had the cooler head of the two. This just might call for a cooler head. Preacher was a deadly man.

Tyler was grinning from ear to ear now. "Thursday, day after tomorrow," he barked. "I'll take the first train out and solve Penfield's little problem. He'd better pay top dollar, too." He frowned. "It didn't say nuthin' about the pay, did it?"

Harvey shook his head and stared out the window. "Maybe I should go," he said, turning back around to face his brother.

Tyler stared at his brother. His jaw dropped. "You!" he barked. "I kin beat you to the draw any day, you know that!"

Harvey nodded slowly. "You can, but Ma always said you ran too hot under the collar. That Penfield is a dangerous man. You got to be careful. Boot Hill is full of guys who could draw fast." He stared at his brother as he let the words sink in.

Tyler laid his knuckles on the desk and leaned in. He bit off his words slowly. "I'm goin' an' that's it." He held his brother's stare for several seconds, then pulled back. "I'll be careful. I won't do nuthin' stupid. I know Preacher is fast." He turned and left, slamming the door shut behind him.

Harvey turned and went back to staring out the window. He couldn't control his brother, he'd learned that a long time ago. He had a bad feeling about this. Tyler had never been tested against the likes of Preacher Dalton.

Tyler cursed under his breath on the way to one of Penfield's saloons. He and Tyler had free beer—that was the arrangement with Penfield. Whiskey, they had to pay for. Tyler dug into his pocket on the way through the door. He would pay today. Beer would not do the job.

Two miners cleared out from the center of the bar as he came through. That calmed him down a little. He had some respect around here. Soon, there would be more. Two whiskeys calmed him down a little more. He left the saloon to pack a few things at the hotel where they stayed. He wouldn't need much, he reflected. This shouldn't take too long.

He'd told Harvey the truth—he planned to be careful. Well, depending on how things went with Preacher. If he got called out, he would answer. He'd heard Preacher liked a straight-up fight in the middle of town. Tyler could do that. He wouldn't be stupid, though. He'd promised Tyler about that, too. The drinks he'd just had would be his last until this was done. He'd need a clear eye.

He wouldn't back down, though. If Preacher wanted a straight-up fight, Tyler would give him one. After that, he would be the king around here. In Silverton, too.

━━━

It was a good morning to move the ore. Deuce had to admit that. The sunlight was just now filtering in over the mountain peaks and through the shade of the pine and aspen trees. The mules and horses were loaded, their breath was steaming in the frosty morning air. They had started loading before sunup—Deuce felt they needed every minute they could get out there riding on the trail before they made camp this evening.

The trouble started before they even got going on the trail. Deuce had seen it coming for a while. McDuffie was a big man, and he was the newest to join the gang. He seemed to think he should be in charge of things. Deuce had seen this kind of thing before. McDuffie was spoiling for a fight. Deuce was just hoping to get down the mountain with the ore before things boiled over.

McDuffie seemed to have a sidekick in a kid named Rooster. That wasn't the name his mama gave him, but the outlaws all called him Rooster. He was a tall, stringy, blonde kid, and he'd shouldered his share of the work. He'd taken to hanging out with McDuffie, who had started griping just as soon as he got up this morning.

Now, just as Deuce was ready to give the order to move out, McDuffie stepped out and confronted him. Rooster stood a few feet back and to the side. The rest of them stayed well back and watched to see how this would turn out.

"This ain't safe!" McDuffie bellowed. He stood inches from Deuce's face. Deuce fought down his anger and returned McDuffie's glare without backing away. He had to get this ore to Durango. After that, he could pay McDuffie off and part ways.

Deuce tried calming the man down. "Okay, what would make you feel safer? Do you want to climb the peaks along the way and scout?"

McDuffie clearly hadn't thought about that. He backed off a few inches and stared at Deuce, his brain working for an answer. "I wanna go out front an' scout from out in front." He gestured behind him. "Rooster here can lead two pack mules, so's I kin do that scoutin' with my rifle handy." He looked around triumphantly. "That'll make all of us safer."

Deuce wasn't very good at poker, but he'd played a lot of it, and he knew how to keep a poker face when he needed to. This was the best possible answer he could have gotten from McDuffie. The truth was, Deuce was worried too, especially in two places they'd used to hold up the miners in the past.

McDuffie was volunteering, downright insisting, actually, to go out in front of the party with Rooster right behind him. Those two would draw any fire that came their way first. The rest of them could hang back and let McDuffie take the worst of it. Deuce struggled to keep a puzzled look on his face, as if he wasn't sure if he liked the idea. Finally, he nodded his head reluctantly.

"Okay," he agreed. "You can...you and Rooster can go out front if you want to. We'll follow behind." His sister's kid nodded. He would agree with anything Deuce said. The third man, named Kyle, who had been with Deuce the longest, nodded as well.

McDuffie hustled off to lead his horse to the front of the column. Rooster fell in behind him. Deuce dropped back and spoke to Kyle in a low tone. "Hang back a little," Deuce advised. "I'll be behind you lookin' out for my sister's kid." He pointed at Pierce, his nephew. "If'n McDuffie does somethin' stupid up there, especially if we're under fire from up above, just skin off'n that horse of yours and git into the brush an' trees. I'll come and find you." Kyle stared, then slowly nodded.

McDuffie mounted his horse up front, raised his arm in the air, and started them off. Deuce kept just a small distance from the front for the first couple hours. They wouldn't be in much danger until then, he felt sure.

Deuce held a pace that kept him close to the rest of the gang for the first several hours. As the sun climbed overhead and they reached the late morning hours, he eased back ever so slightly to let McDuffie's lead increase. He made sure that his nephew Pierce stayed close behind him.

The first of the places they had used for ambush brought Deuce to high alert. He scanned the peaks on either side of the trail anxiously as they passed through without incident. Deuce began to wonder if he had worried about nothing. He could hear McDuffie laughing and swearing loudly up at the front. Deuce shook his head. It was like the man wanted to die.

One hour later, they reached the place where the gang had held up Dugan and two of his friends just a few weeks before. Deuce eased back even farther, listening and watching. When the trail straightened and dipped down into a canyon, he could see McDuffie pulling his horse to a stop. He was yelling and cursing at someone Deuce couldn't see.

While he was watching McDuffie up front, Deuce saw his man Kyle vault from his horse and dash into the trees. He carried his rifle with him, but nothing else. Deuce instantly wheeled his horse into a narrow game path at the side of the trail. He glanced back to see his nephew Pierce hard on his heels. They had covered just a few yards down the path when he heard several rifle shots, followed by the unmistakable boom of a shotgun.

THIRTEEN
MCDUFFIE'S FOLLY

McDuffie had fortified himself with the whiskey in his flask, which was tucked inside his vest pocket. He took a good swig when they turned a corner on the switchback trail, where nobody could see him. Actually, Rooster had been aware of it from the start of the trip, but he knew better than to say anything. When they reached a canyon area with towering peaks on three sides, Rooster wished he had a flask of his own.

McDuffie's vision and his reflexes were both a little slow on account of that whiskey. When he rounded the corner and saw a tall, dark-haired man holding a Winchester on him, he wasn't sure he'd seen things just right. He shook his head to clear his vision, but he saw the same thing afterward. He knew he needed to do something about this, but he couldn't decide exactly what that should be.

He started to bark an order at the man in the trail but stopped short when the guy levered his

Winchester. McDuffie swallowed the oaths forming in his throat and stared at the rifleman. He started to dismount, but that was when the whiskey-fueled courage took over. He swung his rifle up and moved to get a bead on the guy. The last thing he heard was an explosion of gunfire, seeming to come from all sides. The ground rushed up at him.

———

I heard them coming before I could see them. It was hard to believe, but somebody out there on the trail was singing and throwing in a little swearing when he got tired of singing. That went a couple steps beyond the carelessness I'd been hoping for. This guy must have been draining a flask for a while now.

I stepped onto the trail and lifted my rifle. He came around the corner and yanked his horse to a stop, staring down the barrel of my rifle like he couldn't figure out what he was looking at.

"Hands up!" I barked. "Then swing down off that horse nice and easy!"

He stared at me. I could tell he was trying to decide whether he wanted to go along with my command or do something stupid. At the corner of my vision, I could see another horse and rider rounding into the trail, with a couple of pack mules following him. I kept my focus on the guy in front of me. I would have to depend on the others to take care of the second guy.

The man in front of me shrugged, started to lift one leg over the saddle, then changed his mind and swung the rifle toward me. I shot once, knocking him back slightly, then a second shot, coming from above and to the side, drove him sideways. His horse reared, dumping him onto the trail.

Another shot rang out from above on the other side of the trail, followed by the blast of Joanna's shotgun. The second man was blown from his saddle, landing beside his horse with one foot still in the stirrup. His horse trotted a few steps, dragging him behind. I ran up, grabbed the horse's bridle, and held him still, searching the trail behind him for the others. There had to be others. I hoped they weren't as foolish as these two had been. Nobody else needed to die today.

Not wanting to be a target for any others who might be following these guys, I moved over to join Joanna behind the trees and thick brush, listening and waiting. After several minutes, I heard movement, but it came from behind me. After a few more minutes, I heard a whistle. That was Holt, I knew. We'd been through a few scrapes together before this one, so I knew his signal when I heard it.

"Lat!" Holt's voice came from directly behind me.

"Here!" I waved my hand to show him where to find us. He joined us shortly. "There was three more," he said, still trying to catch his breath. "The third one in line jumped off his horse like his pants was on fire and skedaddled into the brush. There was two more behind him, a man and a boy. They both rode off into the brush, too. Might have found them a little game trail or somethin'. I'm sure Sarge has kept an eye on 'em as best he could. Mebbe he can tell us if they've cleared out."

I thought it over. "Too dangerous to trail 'em into

the brush anyway," I decided. "Worse than tracking an injured animal where you can't see him. We'll have to let 'em go if Sarge thinks they've cleared out." Another thought struck me. "What about the pack mules? Did they leave all of 'em out there on the trail when they lit out?"

"Yep," Holt said. "They was all of 'em still out there the last I saw 'em."

After a while, we heard considerable noise coming from one of those northern peaks where I had placed my guys. The noise told me it had to be miners coming down that hill, not a woodsman like Sarge. I waited for Dugan and Barnes to burst out onto the trail.

Dugan spotted the pack horses and broke into a little jig. Reminded me of some kind of dancing bear in a circus or something. He calmed down after a while or else he ran out of breath. I'm not sure which one came first. Trusting Sarge to keep an eye out from above, we rounded up the pack mules. There were four of them, loaded down with a lot of ore and nuggets. I was afraid Dugan would be doing more dancin', but I guess he wore himself out the first time.

When the pack horses were all rounded up, I collected the horses of the two dead men and we slung the bodies over the saddles. I wouldn't leave them out here without a decent burial. Finally, I waved toward the other northern peak, and we waited for Sarge and Otis to come down to join us. I looked at Sarge as he walked up.

"Looks like they taken off into the brush—the three of them might have joined up out there, I couldn't tell. They've only got two horses for three of 'em, and one of those looks like a kid. So, there's two with horses and one on foot. I don't think they'll be comin' after us."

That sounded right to me. I tied one of the dead men's horses to my saddle and the other to Joanna's. The other four divided the pack mules between them, and we set off down the trail to my ranch.

⸻

Deuce kept his roan gelding moving at a trot down the narrow game trail. Branches pulled at his jacket and he occasionally felt one sting his face on the way by. A yelp from Pierce, fighting his way through the branches displaced by his uncle, told Deuce his nephew might be getting the worst of it back there.

He hadn't been close enough to see what had happened to McDuffie, but the number of gunshots he had heard left little doubt he would never see the man again. Unfortunately, he'd had a better view than he'd ever wanted of Rooster when his young life ended. What the shotgun had done to him was something Deuce would never be able to forget. He could only hope Pierce hadn't gotten a view of it. Deuce shook his head. He couldn't understand why either McDuffie or Rooster had raised their guns.

Ten minutes later, he remembered his man Kyle, who had vaulted from his horse and disappeared into the brush, just like Deuce had told him to do. Deuce eased his horse to a halt. He glanced back to see Pierce rein in his horse, just in time to avoid smacking into the rump of Deuce's horse. The kid's eyes were as big as saucers. Deuce decided then and there to put the kid on a train home to his mother just as soon as he could. Before then, though, he had to find Kyle and work his way back to town.

Deuce stared through the underbrush and trees to his east and south, knowing Kyle must be mainly to his east. He couldn't have made good time on foot, so this would involve backtracking some of the ground they'd just covered. Deuce winced when he remembered Kyle was carrying a rifle and likely to be pretty spooked right now. This was a good way to get shot, looking for him in the brush.

If it had been McDuffie out there, Deuce would have left him to take his chances in a heartbeat. Kyle had saved Deuce's bacon a time or two, though, so he heaved a sigh and walked his horse slowly back down the game trail, stopping to listen and watch every fifty feet.

In the end, Kyle came to them. They could both hear thrashing noises in the underbrush coming toward them. Deuce and Pierce moved off the game trail, and they each took cover behind the trunks of cedar trees, taking no chances on showing themselves first. There had been a lot of guns in those peaks, and they didn't yet know for sure who this was.

When Kyle showed himself, Deuce let out a low whistle. Kyle spun, lifting his rifle. Deuce ducked back behind the tree trunk. "Kyle!" His voice was loud enough to carry to any pursuers that might be on their trail, but a rifle shot from Kyle would bring the whole pack down on them in an instant. Kyle recognized the voice, lowered his rifle, and stopped in his tracks. Deuce and Pierce moved out to join him.

They stayed under cover for the rest of the day. It seemed likely the men who had taken back the gold ore had moved on down the trail with their prize, but it wasn't worth taking the chance. Dinner was nothing more than the jerky and biscuits Deuce and Pierce had carried in their saddlebags. Breakfast would be even less. Maybe by mid-morning, they could risk shooting a deer without being heard.

Slumped near a fire no bigger than a hatful, Kyle stared across at Deuce. "It was that big son-of-a-gun, you know? That miner Dugan. I seen him. Who else was it? Who was that feller that stopped us in the trail?"

Deuce shrugged. "I didn't git a look at none of 'em," he admitted. "They was mighty quick with them trigger-fingers."

Kyle fed a few sticks into the fire and said nothing for a while. Deuce huddled under a blanket in the frosty evening air, wondering what he was going to say to Penfield when he had to explain that the whole shipment had been lost. He was more scared of Penfield than he was of the men who'd taken the gold.

It was Pierce who finally spoke. "What do we do now? Go to Silverton? Or Durango?"

Deuce stared up through the trees while he thought. "Silverton," he decided. "We'll have to look for Penfield in Silverton. He was plannin' to make the move from Leadville, an' he's probly done it by now."

Kyle's head came up. "They will know me in Silverton. Dugan, them miners, all of 'em saw me out there on the trail. Mebbe you too. They'll stretch our necks if we show up in town!"

Deuce nodded miserably while he thought about it. "I'll be the one that looks for Penfield when we git to Silverton." He pointed at Pierce. "I'm puttin' you on the train. You'll go back to Californy. Then I'll look for Penfield. If he ain't there, we'll move on to Leadville. Safer there, anyway."

"We move out tomorrow?" Kyle asked.

Deuce nodded. "Yep. We only got two horses fer the three of us, so we'll have to take turns, startin' mebbe mid-morning. I'm guessing we'll hit Silverton day after tomorrow, late afternoon or evenin'. We can camp outside of town."

Deuce reached out to push some dirt over the fire. He rolled onto his back, folded his hands behind his head, and stared up at the stars. He wasn't looking forward to his next meeting with Penfield.

——

We hadn't waited around long in that canyon where we'd stopped the stolen ore pack train. Sarge told me he had spotted three other men coming down that trail, besides the two we had shot. One had jumped off his horse and dashed into the underbrush. We had captured his horse and taken it with us.

There were two more that Sarge had seen pulling over off the trail. That and a few tracks told us they had taken what looked like a game trail, maybe deep into the cover of trees and brush. Maybe they had met up with the third man, maybe not. At best, they had three men and two horses and they were holed up out there somewhere.

I had called a quick meeting and everybody had agreed we should get back to my ranch just as soon as we could. Sooner or later, those folks out there in the woods would have to report back to Penfield or Preacher or somebody. We needed to be off this trail by then. Somebody was bound to come after us.

The pack mules slowed us down some, but we made it to the ranch by nightfall on the second day without anybody giving us trouble on the way. All of us bedded down in the barn or the house and we agreed to make some plans over coffee the next morning.

Over griddle cakes, bacon, and coffee in the morning, we got down to talkin' about where to take this gold, or where to store it while we figured out a way get it to all the miners who'd had it taken from them. That turned out to be tougher to plan than we'd thought because there were still some highwaymen out there who no doubt wanted it back.

We finally decided we had to divide forces to get this done. Barnes felt he could take the stuff that'd been stolen from miners on the Hardrock Hundred Trail, take it up there, and put the word out to some miners. They could get together and figure out how to safely get it to town among 'em. We decided to send two pack mules that way and keep the other two for those who'd had their diggings stolen on the Ice Lake Basin Trail.

Barnes needed help to get up the Hardrock Hundred Trail with two pack mules, so Otis would go with him. After they had dropped that off, Otis would go into Silverton to see what was happening there and report back to us at the ranch. If he could find some of the Ice Lake Basin Trail miners in town and tell them about the rest of the ore still here at the ranch, he would do that.

Dugan would stay here with Holt, Sarge, Joanna, and me to guard the ore still at the ranch and keep an eye out for anybody coming after us. We all had a feelin' those robbers would come after us here.

After we'd seen Barnes and Otis off on their way, we sat down to decide where we could put the other two pack mules' loads of ore until we had a way to divvy it up among those who'd lost it. We didn't want to haul it clear out to the hideout in the cave, and we didn't want to put it in the house or the barn.

We were about out of ideas, staring at the walls and each other, when Joanna snapped her fingers and sat up straight at the kitchen table. We all stared at her and waited.

"When I was a kid," she said, "we always had a root cellar at our house, wherever we were living. It made for good storage in the winter for vegetables and other food, and a good place to go during storms."

I thought that one over. "We didn't see a root cellar around here," I reminded her.

"Did we look for one?" she came back. "There would just be a door of some kind that swings open from the ground. Maybe Jed and his family built one and we just never saw it. We've only been out here a couple times."

Well, that was a better idea than any of the rest of

us had come up with, so we spread out and started looking. It wound up being closer to the barn than the house, which I guess is why I didn't notice it sooner. When I found it, I almost tripped over it.

I hollered and pulled the door open. Sure enough, there were steps leading down. The others came over while I went back to the house for a lantern. Following the steps down, we found some beets, carrots, onions, and potatoes down there, almost with just enough room to store the gold ore we had on the packhorses.

It took the rest of the morning for Holt, Dugan, and me to hump those sacks of ore down into the cellar. Sarge was still a little too stove up from the attack in the saloon, and we flat out refused to let Joanna help. She didn't look too disappointed, I gotta say.

Sarge shot a deer that afternoon and Joanna made some great stew with the venison and some vittles from the root cellar. After dinner, we just had to decide what to do next. We wound up deciding to stay at the house for now while keeping a sharp watch. We hoped nothing blew up before Otis could get back with some news.

In the meantime, though, Joanna and I made a couple of trips to the hideout to be sure we had everything we might need up there, including ammo. Then we all settled down to wait for visitors, friendly or otherwise.

FOURTEEN
MESSENGER

I t was a full two days, plus another half day before Deuce, Kyle, and Pierce reached the outskirts of Silverton. Deuce had fought the urge to push the pace. He knew he'd been outgunned on the trail back there, and he'd counted at least two rifles and a shotgun against them. Plus, there was the guy who'd stopped McDuffie on the trail. The pistol shots must have come from him.

So, they had worked through the trees and underbrush at the side of the trail where they could, moving out onto the trail when the trees and bushes got too thick or the terrain was too treacherous. Deuce had taken the point position himself at those places. Plus, there was the matter of only two horses for three men. That had forced them to go at a walking pace, slowing them down even more.

At the edge of town, all three were hungry, thirsty, and in a foul mood. Deuce gave some money to Pierce, the only one nobody in town was likely to recognize, to go to the café and bring back food for all of them. Deuce wanted a drink pretty bad, but it would cause too much suspicion to have the kid trying to buy whiskey somewhere.

When Pierce came back with the food, they all gulped it down in five minutes flat. Then Deuce sent him back to get some water. After that, he gave the kid money for railroad tickets and told him to find his way back to his mother in San Francisco. Deuce kept the kid's horse and watched while he walked away, heading for the railway station. He felt relief. It had been a bad idea to let the kid come out here in the first place.

Deuce and Kyle retreated a mile out of town and set up camp off the trail and out of sight. Kyle sat down near the campfire and watched while Deuce poked aimlessly at the fire with a stick.

"You seen them tracks leadin' off the trail a few miles back, right?" Kyle asked. "Them boys that took the gold left the trail, headin' east. Looked like pasture land. They taken the gold over there somewhere."

"I saw the tracks," Deuce growled. "They got more guns than we do." He poked at the fire some more. Finally, he couldn't put things off any longer. He moved to his horse and mounted up. "I'm gonna look for Penfield in Silverton and see what he wants to do. I'll get us some vittles while I'm in town." He touched his spurs to his horse and moved away.

The general store was his first stop. Nobody looked familiar as Deuce loaded up some food and ammunition. He had only actually visited Silverton a time or two before now, so he was really only worried about running into Preacher or some of Penfield's gunhands and muscle. And, of course, he had to find Penfield, wherever he was. His brow furrowed up while he paid the shopkeeper and tried to figure out how he was going to do that. He didn't really know if Penfield was here or still in Leadville.

Deuce stepped out of the general store and loaded the items he'd bought into his saddlebags. He looked up and down the street while he did that. There was a saloon directly across from him. It was the Suds 'n Such. Deuce decided that would be his last choice, looking for Penfield. Somebody would know him in there.

Luck finally smiled at him as he stepped back from his horse. Well, it was luck of a kind, but his stomach turned over at the same time. He saw Ike Penfield step out of a bank and cross the street. He moved into a store or shop of some kind when he reached Deuce's side of the street.

Deuce stared down at the gun in his holster and thought about taking it off before he went over to see Penfield. He decided to keep it on. Being unarmed wasn't any kind of guarantee Penfield wouldn't gun him down. Penfield was that kind of man. This way, Deuce at least had a fighting chance. He sucked in a deep breath and moved down to the shop he'd seen Penfield disappear into. The sign said it was some kind of land agent's office.

Deuce knocked loudly, waited a beat, and pushed inside. His eyes swept the office. Only Ike Penfield was in the room. Penfield masked his surprise at seeing Deuce, then he pulled out a chair and sat behind a desk. He placed his hands on the desk. "Well?" he barked.

Deuce walked over and leaned his knuckles on the desk. He hadn't been invited to sit, and he knew better than to sit down uninvited. He believed in breaking bad news fast, though. "We got some of that ore an' stuff," he began. Penfield hadn't blinked. "We was bringin' it down the trail, and we got ambushed." He swallowed loudly. "Bushwhacked," he added unnecessarily. He glanced down to make sure Penfield still had both hands on the desk.

Seconds passed in silence. Penfield slowly leaned forward. "How many? Did they get it all?"

Deuce stared into the coldest eyes he had ever seen, swallowing hard again. "Mebbe five of 'em. They got it all." He spread his hands helplessly and waited. He had expected an explosion, but this was scarier, getting no reaction at all.

Penfield leaned back, never taking his eyes from Deuce. "Where did they go with it?" he intoned slowly. His voice was almost a whisper.

Deuce felt a little hope for the first time. He had an answer for this one. "They left the trail an' cut across a ranch. Mebbe five miles up the trail toward Ice Lake. We didn't have enuff men to go after 'em. They kilt two of my boys in the ambush."

If it bothered Penfield that two of his men had been gunned down, he didn't show it. He rubbed his hands on the top of the desk, still locking eyes with Deuce. He stood slowly, and Deuce backed off a step.

"Where are you staying now? How many men do you have?"

Deuce nodded his head toward the west. "Jest two of us now. We're camped off the trail a little ways about a mile west of town."

Penfield nodded slowly. "I'll meet you there. Tomorrow morning. Make it about ten o'clock. Be ready to move."

Deuce nodded and turned toward the door, counting the steps in his head. When he was through the door and out of Penfield's line of fire, he blew out a long, slow breath. He was still alive. That counted for something.

━━━

Penfield stood behind his desk, drumming his knuckles on the wood. He hadn't shot Deuce for two reasons. One, he had taken over the bank this morning, and that had improved his mood. The president and owner had some objections, but Preacher had put him in jail. After a night or two, Penfield was sure the bank president would see reason.

The second reason he hadn't shot Deuce was that Penfield needed him to guard whatever gold was still up there in the abandoned mine at Ice Lake. That and the fact that it would cause trouble to shoot a man in the back here in town. Even with Preacher acting as the law around here, it would be more trouble than he needed.

Penfield scowled when he thought about Preacher. That was another problem. Penfield left the land office and walked across to the saloon. If there was any news to be had about the ore shipment that had been taken, he might get wind of it in the saloon.

Penfield took a seat in the middle of the saloon, ignoring Preacher's questioning look. He ordered whiskey and settled down into his chair, reminding himself that one of the Boyd twins should get into town tomorrow. That should take care of his Preacher problem.

There were several miners in the saloon—you could tell by how they were dressed. They hung out in groups of two or three at tables scattered around the room. Penfield sipped at his whiskey and watched them. He saw nothing unusual.

After a while, Penfield saw a table of them get up, one at a time, and filter out the door. Puzzled, he watched the other tables. A redheaded kid came up to one of the tables, took their money for the drinks, and spoke briefly. Several minutes later, that table had also emptied and left the saloon.

There was one table of miners left. Penfield swung his gaze back and forth between the miners and the redheaded kid. The kid caught Penfield's stare, ducked his head, and disappeared into the back. The other table of miners didn't look like they were going anywhere.

Penfield left a coin on the table for his drink and moved out to the street. He saw none of the miners who had been in the saloon. The street was quiet. Penfield slammed his fist into a hitching rail in frustration. Something was happening, but he couldn't work out in his head what it was. He stuck his head back into the saloon. The last table of miners had disappeared.

He thought about going back into the Suds 'n Such and choking the redheaded kid until he talked. That would get Preacher into the picture, though. Penfield didn't trust Preacher and didn't want him homing in on this. For that matter, he didn't have anybody else he could trust in this town.

Swearing loudly, Penfield turned and moved on to his hotel room. There was nothing else he could do until he met up with Deuce in the morning.

▭

Otis slouched in his seat at the Silverton café, hat pulled low while he studied the street and sipped at his coffee. He wasn't too worried about being recognized in the town—only Preacher and his old partner Bert would know him around here. Unless, he reminded himself, Ike Penfield had come to town.

After nearly an hour of seeing nothing out there on the street, nursing his third cup of coffee, Otis saw something that made him sit up and stare out the window. Preacher had walked into the jail across the street. Otis knew for a fact Preacher wasn't in the habit of visiting jails. In fact, he avoided them whenever he could.

Otis knew what the sheriff looked like, and that man hadn't been to the sheriff's office and jail this morning. In fact, Preacher was the first and only one who had gone in there. Otis kept watching, and fifteen minutes later, Preacher came out and parked himself on a bench outside the jail. He leaned a rifle against the wall beside him and sipped some coffee. At least, it looked like a coffee cup he was holding. Otis had his doubts whether there was really any coffee in the cup.

After another fifteen minutes, Otis left a coin on the table and slipped out the front door when Preacher leaned his head back against the wall. Maybe, he thought, Preacher was asleep. The pulled-down hat could only do so much to disguise Otis—he was a lot bigger than most folks, and there wasn't much way to hide that. He hurried down Greene Street.

He had his answer to the first question he'd come to town to answer. Who was running the town? The mayor had always been a joke, he was doing what Penfield wanted. The sheriff had at least worn the badge and made some effort at doing the job. He was nowhere to be seen now, and Preacher seemed to have installed himself at the jail. That meant Preacher was the sheriff now, whether or not he had the badge.

Otis had two things he needed to do before reporting back to Latigo Smith and others at Lat's ranch. First, he needed to know if Ike Penfield had come to Silverton. And second, he needed to get word to as many miners as possible that they had recovered some gold ore and had it at the ranch. He wasn't sure right now how to do either, but he suspected he would have to wait in town for a while without being recognized while he figured things out.

There were two places to pick up some news in a town like this. Otis had some experience with this. One would be the livery stable. Whoever ran that place might have an idea about strangers coming into town. Otis frowned for a second, knowing the railroad might have changed things. Still, he felt a lot more comfortable asking the old man at the livery stable. He knew nobody at the rail station, and Penfield might show up at the wrong time over there.

The saloon was the other place to learn some things, but Otis wouldn't be going into there. Latigo Smith, though, had given him a good idea that Otis would definitely try. The kid that worked there washing dishes and carrying out trash could help. His name was Herbie. Herbie trusted Lat Smith and Joanna. Otis would hang out in the back of the saloon and get a message to the kid when he carried out the trash. Otis fingered the note in his pocket, given to him by Joanna. He hoped it would work.

Arriving at the livery stable, Otis found the old man in the back, shoveling out stalls. Otis had left his horse here just a few hours ago. The old man leaned on his shovel and stared at Otis, who cleared his throat and looked around.

"Has there, uh, been anybody new coming in town the last couple days?" he asked.

The old man stared at him suspiciously. "You come in town this mawnin'," he pointed out.

Otis scowled and shuffled his feet. "Yeah, but anybody else?"

The old man shook his head. "Nope." He went back to shoveling.

That just left Herbie and the saloon, and Otis couldn't do much there for several more hours. He looked into a stall piled high with hay. "Could I catch a little sleep in here, Old Timer?"

The old man stopped what he was doing, clearly aggravated at being called Old Timer. He looked at the stall with the hay. "Cost ya sumthin'," he growled.

Otis looked injured. "I paid you good money jest this mornin'," he protested. The old man ignored him and Otis sighed. "What would it cost me, Mister?" he asked.

The old man handed him a shovel and pointed at two stalls. "Shovel out them stalls an' you can have the hay stall without nobody comin' in there the rest of the day."

Otis sighed again, grabbed the shovel, and started earning his nap.

<hr>

Preacher watched Otis walking away down the street without moving from his position. He chuckled to himself. The fool thought nobody would recognize him, wearing that hat. Preacher continued watching from the corner of his eyes as Otis went into the livery stable.

Preacher stretched and stood, walking back into the sheriff's office and jail. Otis didn't bother him much. Preacher had a bigger concern. He didn't for a minute believe Penfield would give up the Suds 'n Such Saloon so easily, or allow Preacher to talk to him the way Preacher had without doing anything.

The baggage handler down at the train station had a new dollar coin in his pocket this morning, along with a description of the Boyd twins. If one or both of them rolled into town, the handler kid would trot right down to the jail and let Preacher know.

Preacher pulled his Colts from the gun belt and checked both to be sure they were loaded. If he were Penfield, that's what he would do—send the Boyds to do the dirty work. Preacher shoved his guns back into the holsters. He was sure he could handle the Boyds. He was just hoping it would be one of them at a time.

When Otis came awake, it was late afternoon and his stomach was growling at him. He stood, stretched, and left the livery stable. After pausing for a moment, he moved on toward the café. Nobody had seen him in there this morning, and it was still pretty early. He felt sure he could eat and get out.

His luck held through a good dinner. Otis left the café, moving almost to the north edge of town before crossing the street and coming down the alley behind the stores. By the time he'd reached a place across from the saloon, evening was falling and the light was fading. Otis pulled his collar up and his hat down, watching to see who would go into the Suds 'n Such. Mainly, he was looking for Ike Penfield.

His patience was rewarded an hour later. By then, Otis was sitting on the ground, leaning against the wall behind him, but he was still watching. The light was still good enough that he could recognize Ike Penfield walking into the saloon. Otis waited for several seconds after Penfield had gone in, then walked back down the alley, crossed the street, and worked his way along until he was concealed in some brush behind the Suds 'n Such.

It was another hour before the kid came out the back of the saloon, hauling a bag of trash. Otis waited until Herbie set the sack down and turned for the saloon before Otis half-rose from his crouched position.

"Hey, kid!" he called in a hoarse whisper. "Herbie! I gotta talk to you. I got a message for you."

Herbie jumped in surprise and darted for the back door of the saloon.

"Wait, kid!" Otis called again. "I got a message for you from Latigo Smith an' his lady...Miss Joanna, I mean." He dug into his pocket and held out a note. "I got a note they sent. I'll set it here on the ground." He put the note on the ground and backed off several paces.

Herbie hesitated, then walked over to get the note, eyeing Otis suspiciously the whole time. Otis held both hands up in the air and waited while Herbie unfolded the note, moved to get some light coming through the saloon window, and read:

Dear Herbie,

   We need some help getting a message to the miners who have been robbed. If there are some miners in the saloon tonight, please let them know they can come to the Latigo Smith ranch to recover some of their money.

   Otis will guide them to the ranch.

Please help.
Joanna Locke
Latigo Smith

Herbie moved across the alley, folding the note. He started to put it in his pocket, then gave it back to Otis instead. "Whaddya want me to do, jest exackly?" he asked.

Otis pointed toward the north end of town. "I'll be there, at the edge of town, waiting," he explained. "Jest tell 'em, one table at a time, that we've took back some of their money that got stolen. Tell 'em Dugan's out there. Tell 'em I've got a lantern and they can follow me to the ranch. They can git some of their stolen money back by mornin'."

Herbie nodded once and started back for the saloon. "I'll tell 'em," he said simply.

FIFTEEN
DIVIDING FORCES

Dugan and I were both in bedrolls on the porch, waiting to see if Otis would bring in any of the miners who'd been robbed. I guess I drifted off to sleep for a while. Dugan claims I was snoring, but I don't believe him. I didn't hear anything.

Anyway, first thing I knew, Dugan was shaking my shoulder and moving over to pick up his Winchester. We heard some riders coming, and we had to make sure they were friendly. The folks we had robbed out there were still looking for us, I was sure of that.

Otis let out a whistle on the way in and Dugan relaxed. I figured they had set that up for a signal ahead of time. I hung out a lantern on the porch and watched as they dismounted and moved in. I counted eight of 'em. Otis told me that was all the miners who had been in the Suds 'n Such.

I waved my arms to get their attention and started by asking who they knew that had been robbed, but wasn't here tonight. They talked among themselves and came up with two more names of miners who had been robbed in the past couple of months.

I explained how we had recovered some of the loot those boys had lost to the robbers, how we thought there was more up the Ice Lake Basin Trail, and that we would look for the rest later. I asked if they thought it would be fair to divide up even-steven what we had now, includin' a share for the two who weren't here. They agreed to that.

We finished up with me explainin' that the ore probably wasn't the safest where we had it right now on the ranch. We had put it all in the root cellar when we got in. I wasn't sure how soon they would come after me, but I pointed at Sarge and Holt, who all of 'em knew from the saloon.

"Sarge and Holt, here, are gonna try to track down the rest of the ore up at the end of that trail, startin' at first light," I said. "We need to get to it before they move what's left. You'll probably want to move what we have outta here at first light, but that will be up to you. Talk among yourselves. Dugan and Otis will go with you and provide a couple extra guns until you get where you're going."

They gathered in front of the porch and went to talkin' among themselves, pointing this way and that. Dugan drifted from one group to the other, answering some questions and no doubt throwing' in his say-so every now and then. Finally, Dugan stepped up to join me on the porch.

"We wanna divide it up even among us, load it up, and move out at first light," he told me. We're takin' it up the Hardrock Hundred Trail, where we can stow it and guard it until we're done with these robbers." He stopped and looked at the house. "You and Miss Joanna gonna be safe here, what with Sarge and Holt goin' up that other trail?"

That was the part that had me a little worried, but I really thought the robbers would go after the rest of the stolen loot first. Sarge and Holt would know to be careful and watch their backtrail. Joanna and I could move to the hideout if we needed to.

I explained all of that to Dugan and told him to watch their back trail, too. Dugan grinned and patted his Winchester. "I barely got off a shot last time, what with all the rest of you folks shootin'. I'll be lookin' for my chance, watching that back trail."

He reached out and patted my shoulder. "Me and the boys will load up the horses," he told me. "We brought a couple pack mules, too. You'd best git some rest. You can git back to yore snorin'."

It was no good tellin' him again I don't snore. He was gone, leading the way to the root cellar. They were moving at first light. Sarge and Holt left right after that, going the other way on the Ice Lake Basin Trail.

I was awake to watch them move out. I stood on the porch, thinking about the things I'd said to Dugan. Maybe, I thought, it would be good if Joanna moved to the hideout today. I could stay behind for just a bit, keeping a sharp eye out for anybody trying to move in. If they did, I could go to the hideout and join her.

Deuce and Kyle had broken camp and been mounted up for nearly an hour now, waiting for Penfield to show up. They held off the trail, allowing a few riders to pass without revealing themselves. Kyle dismounted to give his horse some water, mumbling under his breath while he peered out at the trail.

"What kinda tenderfoot don't git up and git movin' till the day is half gone?" he groused. "We been ready to go for hours. That gold is probly hours down the trail by now if they've took the rest of it."

Deuce wheeled his horse around, ready to tell his partner to shut up, then thought better of it. He needed Kyle on his side, and he didn't know how things were going to shape up today. If Penfield brought a couple more guns to back him up, Kyle might be the only one Deuce could count on.

Kyle glanced at Deuce, nodded, and remounted. He'd gotten the message, even if Deuce hadn't said anything. Ike Penfield was a dangerous man. He'd best keep his yap shut for a while. The horses stamped impatiently, and they waited side-by-side.

Finally, Deuce caught sight of Penfield, trotting around a corner in the trail. Deuce and Kyle moved out to join him. Kyle noted the pistol on the hip and a rifle in the scabbard. Deuce nodded at Penfield but kept glancing back down the trail.

"Don't need nobody else this morning," Penfield growled. "We're gonna look things over and see what they're doin'." He looked at Deuce. "You said four, maybe five of 'em took you down, right?" He didn't wait for an answer. "They're divvying up that gold," he announced with authority. "That means they're gonna be spread out. We just gotta be smart, that's all."

Penfield waved an arm impatiently at the trail and Deuce took the lead, turning a little north when they struck the Ice Lake Basin Trail about an hour later. They rode single file for another hour until Deuce called a halt and dismounted, inspecting tracks joining the trail from the east and turning toward Ice Lake.

Deuce stood after a few minutes and came back to the horses, wiping the dirt from his hands. "Two men with horses, plus two pack mules, I'd say. Short strides, shallow prints. I'd guess the mules are empty." He scowled. "Probly the same mules they taken from us."

"How long ago? How far ahead of us?" Penfield barked.

Deuce stared back at the trail. "Three, four hours, I'd say." He glanced over at Kyle. If they'd started at sunup, those men wouldn't have any lead at all. He knew better than to say so. They both stared at Penfield, waiting.

Penfield stared down the trail, scowling. He had nobody to blame for this one but himself. He thumped his fist against his thigh a few times, then made his decision. He pointed at Deuce and Kyle. "They're goin' for the rest of, if they can find it. You go after them." He dismounted to look at the tracks leading in from the east, then returned to his horse.

"I'm goin' over to look at where they came from," he told them. "Maybe they've still got three or four guns over there at Smith's ranch, but maybe not. It's gotta be Smith who took the gold back, with some guns to back him. Maybe they split up the gold and left Smith there by himself." He mounted and rode east.

———

Sarge and Holt were moving at sunup, leading two pack mules away from Latigo Smith's ranch house. They moved quickly across the pastureland leading to the Ice Lake Basin Trail, not concerned yet about being followed or running into any of the thieves they had left behind.

At the Ice Lake Basin Trail, they slowed only slightly, rifles at the ready as they rounded bends on the trail. After thirty minutes of moving west and north, Sarge pulled them off at a rise in the trail and pulled a long brass cylinder from his saddlebag.

"What's that thing?" Holt thought he knew the answer already but watched and started chuckling when Sarge extended the length of it, held it up to a tree, and put his eye to the end of it.

"Spyglass," Sarge growled. "Still works too, just as good as it did when my pappy used it in the navy."

Holt left off laughing while Sarge studied their backtrail. After a few minutes, he snapped the spyglass shut and returned it to his saddlebag. They pushed forward, knowing they could make good time until they reached the canyon where they'd had taken back the miner's gold. The stash with the rest of it, if there was one, could only be beyond that point.

By noon, they had reached the canyon and stopped to pull a little food from their packs, washing it down with water from their canteens. Sarge moved off to check the backtrail again, and they moved on, stopping only to water the horses and mules when they crossed a mountain stream.

Moving past the canyon area, Sarge dismounted and studied the trail. He stood and followed the trail on foot for several yards before returning to the horses. "Ain't had rain in a while, so there's some tracks," he mused. "Too many of 'em and they're too shallow. Could be them boys we relieved of the gold, but hard to tell." They pushed on.

Going was slower now as they pulled off to examine any side trails that could lead to a cave or abandoned mine in the rock faces just off the trail. Holt could tell Sarge was growing more uneasy as the afternoon wore on, stopping more often to check the backtrail. If anybody was coming after them, they could close ground in a hurry now.

Afternoon shadows were lengthening when they stopped after a long climb up the trail. Holt dismounted and waited, knowing Sarge was going to put that spyglass to use again. Holt tethered the horses and trailed behind Sarge, waiting while Sarge scanned the trail below them. Holt came to attention when he heard an unhappy snorting noise. Sarge snapped the spyglass shut and continued staring down the hill.

"I think there's dust down there," he said finally. "We could've picked up some folks tailin' us up here." Holt said nothing and waited. Sarge looked up at the sky, then back at the trail. "Looks like we might get some rain tonight," he said. He started to smile. "Let's pull off and make camp for tonight," he said. "Mebbe we can turn them that's doin' the hunting into the ones that's gettin' hunted by mornin'."

⎯⎯⎯

Tyler Boyd looked balefully out the window on the ride up to Silverton. He'd been on this train before, and who cared about looking at the mountains, anyway? He was about to make a name for himself and make a lot of money while he was at it. His brother Harvey might be better at running things in Leadville and making Ike Penfield happy, but Tyler figured he would be the biggest man in Colorado after he took down Preacher.

He'd seen Preacher fight, and he was good, but Tyler was faster. Men went down when Preacher started firing, but that was because they were scared. Tyler had seen it. Twice, as a matter of fact. When they saw that gun come level, they were backing away. They saw it coming and went a little pale around the gills. Well, Tyler was faster. He was sure of it. He wouldn't be scared.

Now he looked out the window, but he wasn't seeing any of the sights. He grinned. Ike Penfield was going to need him, but did he really need Penfield? He could be the boss. His brother Harvey could work for him. They would make a great team.

Somewhere along the way, Tyler drifted off to sleep. He came awake when there was a loud hiss and squeal as the train came to a stop in Silverton. Tyler grabbed his bag and stepped down to the platform, then followed a couple other passengers out into the street in Silverton. He saw a kid who worked for the railroad dart out from behind him and trot down to a saloon. He didn't think about that much. People got thirsty, didn't they?

Tyler stopped and looked at the second telegram that had come in just yesterday. Harvey had given it to him before he left, along with warning him about being smart, or careful, or something. Tyler snorted. Harvey was too much like their mother.

Another look at the telegram told him he should look for Ike Penfield at some land agent's office. He moved along Greene Street, reading the signs. He looked regretfully at a saloon as he passed it. He would have to come back here after he'd finished the business he had come to Silverton to do.

Now he spotted the land agent's office, knocked, and pushed the door open. It looked empty. He called Penfield's name once, then twice, but got no answer. Tyler left, pushing the door back open and moving out to the street, shaking his head in frustration. He would have to go looking for Penfield now, before he tangled with Preacher. Not quite how he had pictured things.

━━━

Joanna was standing behind me in the yard next to the barn, watching me do something she had never seen me do before. I could almost feel her worry and the questions she wanted to ask, even though I couldn't see her.

I lined up six glass bottles on a log, feeling the weight of my Colt .45 where it was strapped down against my leg. I walked off about forty paces and faced the bottles, then drew my gun and fired. I made sure to pull it smoothly and clear the leather of the holster before I brought it level. I crouched and fired six times, then looked at the bottles. Five were broken. One still stood on the log. I shook my head a little and returned the Colt to the holster.

"Are you fast?" The voice sounded like it came from a long way behind me. I turned to look at Joanna.

I nodded my head just a little. "I'm fast," I said. "Faster than most, I'd say. Not as fast as a few, but I hit what I aim at." I turned and looked at that bottle still standing on the log. "Usually," I corrected myself. "I need to practice a little more."

"Okay." Her voice still sounded small and far away. She turned and walked back to the house.

I moved back to the log and put up five more bottles beside the one that was still standing, then reloaded the Colt. Thirty minutes later, I decided to take a break for a while. I needed to talk to Joanna.

I found her in the kitchen, staring out the window. I walked up to put my hands on her shoulders, and she turned around to wrap me up in a hug.

"Is it that Preacher guy?" she asked. "Penfield? Who do you think you have to practice for?"

I leaned back a bit and shook my head slowly. "I don't know," I admitted. "Maybe one of them, maybe somebody else. I don't know." I heaved a sigh and stared out the window over her head. "What I know is that some bad men want more money than they've already got, and they want it pretty bad. And they know they have to go through me to get it."

We stood for a long time without talking, then I stepped back to hold her shoulders again. "I think you have to go to the hideout now," I told her. "I'll be up there in a little while, myself. There's just a couple things I have to do here first. I'm afraid that a few of those guys are coming to the ranch. Maybe Sarge and Otis or Dugan will get back first, but maybe not. We're safer up there."

She sighed and walked to the corner of the kitchen to pick up a bag she had packed just that morning. I walked her out to the corral, and she watched as I saddled her horse. I helped her up, and she leaned over to give me a kiss. When she had ridden out of the corral and started on the path through the upper pasture, I walked back over to the log and reloaded the Colt.

<hr />

Ike Penfield worked his way east from the Ice Lake Basin Trail, feeling uneasy about things. He usually had a gunman or two to do his dirty work for him, and he considered himself to be on enemy territory here. He held to draws in the land and stream beds where he could, trying to stay out of view.

After forty-five minutes, he stopped to water his horse in a stream, then slowly walked the horse close to the top of a rise. He left his horse and finished the climb to the top of the rise, then laid down to look things over. He could see a couple of buildings down there, then he heard gunfire.

Puzzled, Penfield froze where he was, then

crawled back down to his horse to get his binoculars from the saddlebag. He crawled back to the top and trained his glasses first on the house and barn down there. He saw a man drawing and firing his pistol at some bottles on a log. He snickered. Practice was for tinhorns and fools.

Motion to his left caught his eye, and he swung the binoculars to get a better look. It was a woman! Penfield lowered the binoculars, stared in that direction, then raised the glasses again. He was right the first time. It was a woman, riding away from the house.

Penfield crawled back down toward his horse, a grin splitting his thin, cruel mouth. If Smith had a wife or girlfriend riding out to the hills by herself, he could take advantage of that. This was the kind of thing that made a man vulnerable. He had Latigo Smith where he wanted him.

SIXTEEN
TYLER BOYD

They had rigged a tarp under a towering cedar tree, so when the claps of thunder and flashes of lightning began around midnight, Sarge just smiled a little in the darkness. He knew the hard rains would come soon, washing out the tracks down there on the trail. He rolled back up in the blankets and drifted off to sleep. A lifetime habit would have him awake before dawn, ready to watch his pursuers from the rocky peak above this position.

Sunlight was peaking over the mountaintops to the east when Sarge, settled down to watch, moved his spyglass just slightly. He adjusted the lens a little to get a better view of the two men down below who were trying to make sense of the trail in front of them. After ten minutes of casting back and forth, one of them motioned to the other, and they remounted.

Catching up the reins to their pack mules, the two men proceeded forward on the trail. Sarge grinned with satisfaction and snapped the spyglass shut. Time to wake up Holt. Sarge chuckled. Holt had some bark on him, Sarge had to admit, but he'd developed a bad habit of sleeping past sunrise after he'd started running that saloon. Sarge intended to fix that problem.

―

Deuce had been worried about this since the thunder and lightning had started up last night. There had been a downpour for about an hour after that, soaking his bedroll and making his mood even worse than it had been for the last couple of days. Kyle stood off to his left, muttering curses and staring down the trail. Deuce tried to ignore him.

Deuce took a quick look around, then folded his arms across his chest and tried to sort out what they would do next. He'd had the feeling for a couple days now that Penfield might just be setting them up as the prime targets at a turkey shoot.

Starting with that trip last week to get a shipment of ore, for instance. They'd needed at least two more men than they'd had, mostly for scouting. A couple guys out front, scouting all the places on the trail where they could get held up, just like Deuce and his boys had done to the miners. They had just been targets when they'd hit this canyon.

Deuce took another uneasy glance at the surrounding peaks. Whatever they did, they'd best not stand out here in the middle of the trail like a couple of fools. He motioned at Kyle, who didn't even see him while he stared down the trail and muttered a few curses and threats.

"Kyle! Mount up!"

That got his attention, at least. Kyle turned, took two steps, and mounted. Deuce had the feeling maybe Kyle didn't have Deuce's back on this trip. Deuce led the way forward. No use looking for tracks now, and they couldn't worry if they were being followed to the old mine where the rest of the booty was. Penfield had gone off on some mission of his own and left them out here. Every man for himself. Deuce just wanted to get to that stash of ore and get out.

Another day of pushing forward found them climbing up past nine thousand feet. They made camp again, and now Deuce was barely taking the time to check his backtrail for pursuit. He woke at dawn, shivering as he threw off his blankets and stamped his feet down into his boots.

Deuce boiled some water and made a brew he called coffee. Kyle had another name for it, but Deuce really didn't care. He'd decided that he and Kyle would part ways after this trip. Deuce walked over and prodded Kyle with his boot until his partner came awake and growled at him.

By the time Kyle had finished complaining about the coffee, Deuce had mounted and was waiting to move on. He took a minute to explain his plan before leading the way out.

"We oughtta be at the cave in a couple hours," he said, straining to see the trail in front of him as the steam from his breath blocked the view. "We load up them mules for a few hours, then come right back here to camp tonight."

Deuce glanced sideways at Kyle, who nodded sullenly. That seemed to Deuce like as much agreement as he was going to get. He shrugged and kicked his horse in the ribs. He was just hoping for the day to get a little warmer as the sun rose.

He was right on the money, as far as when he'd said they would get to the cave. Deuce reined in his horse and waited for Kyle to pull alongside. They led their horses into a thick stand of pine trees to the side and returned on foot, pistols drawn, looking for any sign of visitors to the abandoned mine since they'd left. Satisfied they were alone, after scouting the area and looking inside, they returned to bring the pack mules as far as they could, leading them into the mouth of the abandoned mine.

The work was back-breaking, just like it had been before. Deuce was having to do the hauling this time, though. He had brought a few extra burlap bags, and they knew now just how much weight those bags could take before tearing. They took countless trips before taking a break to chew some cold biscuits and jerky, then went back to hauling the ore. Both slipped and fell on the icy path several times.

When the mules were loaded, Deuce went to get the horses. He took the saddlebags from both and tossed one to Kyle. "Load some into the saddlebag. Not too much," he added needlessly. "Then we're outta this place." He looked back over at Kyle. "If you come across a nugget or two that looks real good, mebbe it could wind up in yore pocket." Kyle smiled for the first time that day. They turned for one last trip into the abandoned mine.

When they came back with the saddlebags filled, they each slung the bag over their horse and led them out. Deuce had one foot in the stirrup when he heard a sound he'd heard before. It was the sound of a rifle being cocked. He looked behind him at Kyle, who'd heard it, too. And Deuce could tell that Kyle was getting ready to do something really stupid.

Sarge wondered once in a while if they were being set up for an ambush. It didn't seem like it should be this easy. They didn't have to stay too close to the men up front—the muddy trail made the tracks plain. Whoever they were, they seemed to just move forward at a steady pace. If the robbers were stopping to check their backtrail, they wouldn't be making this much progress.

In the late afternoon, Sarge and Holt slowed their pace, not wanting to stumble into their quarry's campsite in the fading light. That would make for a fast trip to Boot Hill. With maybe an hour of daylight left, they stopped and made camp. Picking up the trail again at daybreak should keep them close enough. The increased elevation and the bite from an icy wind told Sarge they were getting close to the stolen gold. Ice Lake couldn't be too far ahead.

After a quick breakfast at dawn, they were back on the trail. Stopping only to water their horses, they kept on until close to noon. Sarge was growing uneasy about stumbling into their quarry, then he heard a faint noise. They halted and listened, staring down the trail. No doubt about it, what they were hearing was the sound of men cursing.

Sarge chuckled and pulled his Winchester from the scabbard. They moved forward, edging slowly around two bends in the trail until they saw the two men they'd been following, leading their horses from what looked like the mouth of a cave.

Sarge was a man of few words, and he'd found that the sound of him cocking his Winchester got attention faster than any fancy words he'd ever been able to come up with anyway.

Sure enough, the man in front froze in his tracks when he heard Sarge racking the Winchester. The second guy, though, either hadn't heard the noise, or he'd been the slowest kid in his class at school. He reached forward and yanked his rifle from the scabbard.

Sarge fired just as the man's horse reared, sending the outlaw backward. He landed out of Sarge's view as the horse reared again, then crow-hopped away. Sarge fired a second time as the outlaw came to his knees, lifting his rifle. Sarge heard Holt's first shot at the same time that Sarge triggered his second.

Both shots struck the outlaw full in the chest. He pitched backward and landed face up. The horse bolted down the trail, jumping over the fallen gunman as he did. Sarge remembered the other man and swung his rifle to cover the second outlaw, who hadn't moved. His hands were in the air as he sat motionless at the side of the trail.

Sarge moved forward, rifle at the ready. "Back away from your horse!" he barked. The man did so. When Sarge commanded him to slowly remove his pistol and drop it, he again did what he was told. He laid face down while Sarge tied his hands behind his back.

Sarge rose and swung around to look at Holt, who had gone to check on the outlaw they had shot. Holt stood and shook his head. "Dead," he said simply.

Sarge looked at the man on the ground, then helped him to his feet. "What's your name?" he asked.

The outlaw stared at him, then looked away. "Folks call me Deuce," he mumbled. Sarge pushed him toward his horse.

"Well, Deuce," Sarge told him, "we're gonna bundle you up all nice and tight, then we're gonna take a ride back to town." He pointed at the dead man. "What was his name?"

The man shook his head and spat on the ground. "His name was Kyle," he growled. He shook his head. "Allus was a hothead and a fool, he was."

Holt had retrieved the dead man's horse by then, so he and Sarge tossed the dead body over the horse and tied the man's hands and feet underneath. Sarge straightened up and saw the loaded pack mules standing near the edge of the trail.

"Well now, ain't that nice?" he said. "All loaded up an' ready to go. This here has been what we call a profitable trip."

═══

Tyler Boyd stood outside the land agent's office, trying to think where else Ike Penfield might be in this town. He saw a saloon down the street, but he decided against looking in the saloon. That was the kind of place Penfield would want to own, if he didn't own this one already. Penfield didn't spend a lot of time in saloons, though. He just took money from them. Besides, that might be where Preacher was spending time. Boyd didn't want to meet Preacher in there. Preacher might have some kind of advantage in the saloon.

Looking in the other direction, he saw a bank. That seemed likely. Boyd crossed the street and stepped into the bank. A teller greeted him with a bright smile. Boyd stepped across to the teller's cage.

"Can I see Mr. Penfield?" he asked.

The teller's smile faded. "He...uh.. Mr. Penfield isn't in this afternoon," she stammered. "I don't know where he is."

Boyd stared at her, his eyes narrowed. She was flushed and she was avoiding his gaze, but he thought she was probably telling the truth. Others in the bank were staring at him now. He didn't want to draw attention like this. Not yet, anyway. He turned and left the bank.

Boyd pulled a watch from his vest pocket. Noon. He walked down the street until he saw a sign for a café. He ducked into the café and took a seat by the window. When a waitress came, he ordered steak and a coffee without looking at her.

Three coffees later, Boyd was still staring out the window. He knew he would recognize Preacher if he saw the guy. Tall, thick build, bushy black eyebrows and mustache, and always the battered black hat. Boyd had been thinking this over. He wanted to meet Preacher out there in the street. It looked like this might be Preacher's town now. Everybody would have to know this was a fair fight.

The waitress had stopped coming around to fill up his coffee cup. Boyd looked around to get her back over, then turned back to the window. Something had caught his attention across the street at the saloon. Boyd stared as Preacher stepped out of the saloon, stopped to light a cigar, then moved out to the street.

Boyd dropped a coin on the table, leaped to his feet, and turned to leave. He bumped the waitress as he left. She yelped with pain as the coffee sloshed from the pot and burned her hand, but Boyd paid no attention to that.

Yanking open the café door, Tyler Boyd stepped out onto the street. Preacher was coming his way and was maybe forty feet away now. Perfect, Boyd thought. Just what I need.

"Preacher! I'm calling you out." Boyd was surprised at how high-pitched his own voice sounded.

Preacher stopped and stared at Boyd, looking him over from head to foot as he switched his cigar from his right hand to his left.

"I know you," Preacher said. His voice was calm and puzzled, like he was trying to solve a riddle of some kind. "Wait, I know," he said, snapping his fingers. "From Leadville, you and your brother..."

Too late, Boyd realized he'd been distracted. Preacher was drawing! Panicked, Boyd's hand dropped to his gun, and he started his draw. Preacher's first shot whined past his ear and Boyd grinned as his own gun came level. He snapped off a shot and saw Preacher wince. *Shoulder*, Boyd thought, *I grazed his shoulder*.

Boyd steadied his aim for the next shot. Time seemed to pass ever so slowly as he dropped his aim just slightly. He felt the impact of Preacher's next bullet before he heard the shot. There was a tremendous blow to his stomach. Boyd stared down, then stared blankly at Preacher. Something was wrong. His legs were getting weak.

The next blow was to the middle of his chest. His gun slipped from his fingers. He was lying on his back somehow, staring up at the blue sky. He heard voices and wasn't sure where they were coming from. Then the light faded away.

━━━

Preacher sat in the chair behind his desk at the saloon, shirt off, while the town doctor treated his shoulder. It was the only shot Tyler Boyd had gotten off, but it was a lot more painful than Preacher would have thought. He'd been in several gun battles, but he usually saw to it that he had just a slight edge. Today, he'd had none.

His enforcement crew was in the office with him— Bert and Blondie. They were watching, so Preacher clenched his jaws shut and said nothing while the doctor sewed up the furrow plowed by Boyd's bullet.

He stifled the sigh of relief he felt when the doctor was done and waited to speak until they were alone in the office. Preacher tried to set aside the doubts he was feeling about himself for the first time. Had he slowed down now that he wasn't a kid anymore? Others, like Bert here, had done his fighting in recent years.

He became aware the others were watching him while he just stared at the desk. Preacher pulled himself together to get down to business.

"That kid was in Leadville, worked for Penfield up there," he said. "Had a twin brother...what's that name?"

"Boyd." It was Bert that gave him the answer. "Dunno his first name. No sign of the brother so far. I checked over there at the rail station. Just that one you kilt come in on the mornin' train."

Preacher nodded absently, still thinking about how close that bullet had come. "What about Ike Penfield?" he asked. "I ain't seen him around here all day."

Blondie spoke up. He'd been in the Suds 'n Such last night, picking up on snatches of the conversation. He'd wanted to make some money on what he'd heard in there, but he didn't have any good ideas on how. That was the normal thing for Blondie, not having good ideas.

"Penfield had a few guys retrieving some o' that gold they stole from the miners," he said, feeling more important after spilling that news. "They was talkin' about it out there last night," he continued, jerking his head toward the saloon floor. "That big guy, Dugan, wasn't in there, but somebody must've told them about it, 'cause that's all they seemed to be talkin' about."

"And?" Preacher shifted forward in his chair, wincing at the pain that motion caused him.

Blondie, thrown off track, stopped to get his story together. "Well," he said, picking up steam again, "I trailed 'em. They was leaving here a few at a time. I trailed the last group."

Blondie let that sink in, but Preacher's impatient stare got him talking again. "They met up out there, then they rode to that rancher's place. The one that shot my partner, I mean. Latigo Smith. I didn't get close enuff to hear or see nothin' out there."

Preacher stared out the window while he absorbed that. He swung back to stare at Blondie. "Are you sayin' that Penfield took some boys to go and get that gold back?"

Blondie hadn't actually thought of that before now, but it made sense. He nodded. "That's what I'm thinkin'," he said importantly.

Preacher nodded. "We stay here," he announced. "We don't go after them, but we'll be ready when they show up in Silverton again. That includes the brother of that guy I shot today. He'll likely show up when he finds out I plugged his brother."

Bert and Blondie looked at each other doubtfully. "You just wanna wait?" Bert finally asked.

Preacher stood and reached for his hat. "You boys were too young to fight in the war," he said, staring down at them. "I fought in Longstreet's corp. He believed in good ground. 'Make your fight on good ground,' that's what he always said." He waved an arm at the saloon, then swung it in a bigger motion to show the town. "This here," he announced, "is good ground."

SEVENTEEN
HUNTING AND HUNTED

For a while, Penfield stayed very cautious. He held to the low ground where he could, worried that the woman would see him moving at the edges of her vision. He pulled over at the next slight rise he found, training his binoculars on her as she moved and studying what she carried on the horse. After a few minutes, he was satisfied that she had only a pistol—she wasn't carrying a rifle in her hands, and he couldn't see one in a scabbard on the horse.

Penfield rose and moved back to his horse, staying in a crouch. This was starting to look easy. She didn't have a rifle, and she wasn't checking her back trail. He should be able to ride right in and take her prisoner. Even if she could use that pistol, he could pin her down with rifle fire. Maybe Latigo Smith would part with this ranch for a song to get the woman back.

He paused beside his horse and studied her through the binoculars for a while before remounting.

She was headed in a direct line for a notch in the mountains. He grinned. She still wasn't checking behind her for pursuit. She felt comfortable on Smith's property. Penfield would change all that.

Mounting, he turned his horse north and rode to the edge of the mountains, moving slowly, then picking up his pace as she climbed into the notch. He had lost sight of her as she climbed, but she also wouldn't be able to observe him. He paused one more time to carefully mark the spot where she had disappeared into the notch, then pushed on.

Half an hour passed before he reached the notch, but he was feeling confident she hadn't seen him. She hadn't been checking her back trail. Penfield dismounted and stayed low, moving forward in a crouch. He struck a trail in another few minutes, winding up into the mountains. Penfield straightened up and studied the trail and the ground in front of him. Better, he decided, to take it on foot. He could see the tracks—she had ridden up here, but better for him to take it slow and stay out of sight for a while longer.

Returning to his gelding, Penfield led him into a stand of cedar trees and tethered him. He pulled his rifle and a box of ammunition from his horse and filled his pockets with the ammo. He lifted his canteen from the saddle horn, hung it around his neck, and turned to retrace his steps to the trail he'd found. On second thought, he returned, reached into his saddlebag, and pulled a little food from it. This might take a while if she had a good hiding spot up there.

When he reached the trail again, Penfield squatted,

cradling his rifle across his lap. Staring up to either side of the winding trail, he saw mostly a rocky face with some cedar and pine trees growing in small stands, broken by brush and rocky scree. That could be some treacherous footing. His gaze returned to the trail, and he shook his head.

Even though he hadn't seen a rifle, if she wised up to the fact he was on her trail, all she had to do was take cover behind a good-sized boulder and pick him off with her pistol when he came around a bend. That's if he took the trail up. He shook his head again. Maybe she could shoot, maybe she couldn't. He wasn't willing to take that chance.

It didn't seem to matter which side of that trail he chose, the footing looked about the same on either side. He chose the left. It was slow-going, hard work, made worse by the fact he had to keep his head down and stay low to the ground. In fifteen minutes, he was pouring sweat and swearing under his breath as he worked from tree to tree and boulder to boulder. He stopped and mopped his face with his bandanna while he peered up the slope.

This had to go faster. The girl could have climbed over the top and gone halfway to Canada by now. There was another boulder offering cover, maybe fifteen yards straight in front of him. Penfield grasped his rifle with his right hand and pushed off a boulder with his left, scrambling up the slope.

Disaster struck when he was just five feet short of reaching a large boulder he was aiming for. He was leaning forward, reaching for the boulder with his free hand, when his foot came down on some loose shale.

It gave way as he tried to grab the edge of the boulder.

His footing gone, Penfield tumbled and rolled down the slope, slamming up against the boulder he'd been using for cover just a minute before. His breath left him in a whoosh and he cried out for just a second from the pain of his shoulder slamming into the rock.

Penfield clapped a hand over his mouth, thankful that his Winchester hadn't slipped from his grip. The pebbles and small rocks he'd dislodged tumbled down the incline below him, making a surprising amount of noise.

Penfield scrambled around behind the boulder, using it to shield him from wherever she was, up there above him. He remained still, grabbing at his shoulder and waiting for the noise from the mini-slide he'd created to die down. He stared overhead, waiting for a gunshot that didn't come. Had she heard him?

Joanna reached the cave with no trouble. She was a little relieved, having worried about whether she would remember when it was time to leave the trail and move west to the hideout. As it was, she found it without having to cast back and forth. The crude corral they had built to the side was intact. She turned her horse into the corral with some food and water.

The guns were where she had left them. She moved both the Winchester rifle and the shotgun closer to the mouth of the cave. A quick check told her both had been loaded. She pulled boxes of ammunition closer and went to check on the firewood they had stored inside. It was there—dry and ready to use.

Now that she was here and had a chance to think things over, it bothered her she hadn't been checking behind her on the way up. What if she had been followed? She moved out to the trail and crouched behind the boulder that had been her landmark on the way up. She saw no activity down there.

Feeling better, she moved back to the cave and checked the food they had on hand. Moving to the back, she positioned some of the firewood and laid the supply of matches alongside, ready to start a cooking fire. The smoke would filter out the hole at the top and disperse among the trees and brush above.

Moving back toward the entrance, her eyes fell on an old broom at the side. Lat must have left it there, she thought. More to keep herself busy than anything else, she swept the twigs, dust, and brush toward the entrance. Finishing up at the mouth of the cave, she swept the debris away from the entrance, then moved back to the boulder she was now using as a lookout spot.

She shaded her eyes with her hand, staring down the trail and looking for any movement she could see. Latigo had said he would be up here in a while, but maybe this was too early for him to get here. She turned to go back to the cave when she heard a noise. Joanna froze where she stood. That had sounded like a small slide of rocks below! She broke into a trot, going back to get both the rifle and shotgun.

Crouching behind the boulder again, Joanna laid the Winchester across the top and settled herself down to watch for movement. The rifle would be better at this range than the shotgun. That couldn't have been Lat—he would have called out to her. No, this would be an unwelcome visitor. She reproached herself again for not having been more careful on the way up.

Nothing she could do about that now, she told herself. She needed to see him before he saw her. The thought of several attackers was too much to deal with. She would concentrate on one at a time.

The trail wound out of view about fifty yards below, and it was too much to hope he would come up on the trail, anyway. She concentrated on watching for movement from the corners of her eyes at the sides of the trail.

In about five minutes, she thought she saw something. It was on the west side of the trail, and she was sure she had seen a branch move. That could be an animal, but it could be a man. Joanna kept her gaze on the place where she had seen movement, then slowly searched the areas at both sides.

There! It looked like a patch of black where it didn't belong. The trees and brush were green, the rocks and shale were gray. Black didn't fit in this picture. She rose and brought the rifle sights to bear, then stopped. A shot would give away her position. Did she want to do that without a clear view of what she was aiming at?

The thought that there could be multiple attackers made her decision easier. If there was more than one attacker down there, she needed help. Latigo was the only one who could help her. Would he hear a rifle shot from up here if he was still at the ranch? Joanna thought he would. She had to try.

She settled back down behind the boulder, sighting in on that patch of black. He moved just a little, and she could see the outline of a man. Joanna held her breath, then exhaled slowly as she squeezed. The patch of black disappeared, then she heard noises again. That sounded like what she heard before. She hoped it was the sound of someone tumbling down the mountain.

The bullet burned across his shoulder, and Penfield cried out in surprise at the pain. Knocked off balance, he slid back down once again to the boulder below. He lost his grip on the rifle but was lucky enough to grab it before it slid past him. Not sure if he was still in somebody's sights, he sprinted back up the slope, moving around the boulder and rushing to reach a place he'd seen before—a spot that offered excellent concealment.

There was a rocky face in front of him now, with a few scattered boulders behind. He was confident he would be shielded by fire from above by the rocky face. If that gunshot brought anyone from below, the boulders at his back would offer protection. If only he could get there.

He lunged forward and charged up. He was almost there now. He reached the first of those boulders he wanted to have at his back and ducked as he raced around it. Another gunshot sounded from above, and rocky chips tore into his face as he rounded the boulder.

Penfield swore heartily and dove for the protection of the rocky face. He rolled and tucked himself at the foot of the cliff face, then propped himself against it as he checked his injured shoulder. It oozed blood, but it was only a deep graze. He tore his shirt sleeve with his teeth and used it to stop the bleeding. Worried about another shot from above, he squeezed himself against the rock face.

Penfield looked overhead at the sun. There were a few hours of daylight left. She'd had a rifled stowed away up there somewhere, that seemed obvious now. He cursed himself for not having thought of that sooner. Another frontal attack in broad daylight would be stupid, and Penfield prided himself on not being a stupid man. He would wait for darkness and keep an eye out below while he waited. Darkness would be his friend. He would get her then.

———

I had finished practicing with my Colt and now I was thinking it was time to follow Joanna up into the hills. The few cows Jed had left behind when he sold me the property were doing fine out in the lower pasture. I ducked into the root cellar and found that Dugan and boys had carried away all the ore and left things in good shape.

Stepping into the corral to catch up my horse, I heard a gunshot. I froze, staring up into that notch in the hills. Moments later, there was another shot. I started for my horse, then stopped and ran back to the house, coming out with a pair of moccasins. I'd owned a pair since I was a boy in this country, and I'd learned how to be noiseless in the woods. It made the difference between coming home with meat for the table or not.

I left the corral at a gallop, then slowed my horse down to think things out a little. There was food in the cave, so Joanna had no reason to shoot unless she was under attack. I had to figure somebody else was up there, and it wasn't a friend.

There were lots of problems for me going in, though—who was shooting at who up there? How many were there besides Joanna? I would have to guess she was at the hideout or near it. She'd had enough time to get there. If she wasn't at the hideout by now, I wouldn't have any idea where to start.

As I moved toward the notch in the hills, I swung my horse to point a little west of it. Trouble most likely came from there. The Ice Lake Basin Trail was over in that direction. I'd seen little traffic coming from the other side. I would rather come in behind some unfriendlies than ride right into them.

After I'd swung far enough west, I breathed a little easier and worried a little less about drawing fire from above me. I gradually turned north and found some protection and cover from the trees leading up into the mountains. From there, I turned east and rode along toward the trail I knew Joanna had taken. Mostly, I concentrated on the ground in front of me, looking for tracks. It didn't take long to find some.

The tracks were off to my right. Whoever he was,

he'd ridden a little more out in the open than I was doing now. There was only one set of tracks, to my relief, but as I pulled up to study them, it seemed to me he might have seen Joanna move into the notch. From where he'd sat, nothing would have blocked his view if she had been out there in front of him.

I pulled up to think this one through again, listening for any sounds of movement. It was quiet as death, other than the occasional bird call. I moved my horse forward slowly, still listening and also watching those tracks to my right. In another hundred feet, the tracks crossed in front of me and moved into the trees. Minutes later, I found a horse tethered in the trees.

I didn't waste a lot of time. He'd left on foot, I could see that from his boot tracks, so I cut his horse loose and gave him a slap on the rump. It would at least slow the attacker down if he got away from me and came through here. I led my horse uphill and deeper into the tree line before I tied him to a tree and swapped out my boots for the moccasins. I returned to follow the boot tracks. Now's when all that hunting I'd done as a boy would pay off. Just one difference this time, I thought. I was hunting a man now.

The silence had me puzzled. One of 'em had a view of the other one. A good enough view to take a shot, anyway. I was betting Joanna had the high ground. She'd had enough time to climb up there before I heard the shot. If she had the high ground and had been the one to take a shot, maybe she had him pinned down. That was a lot of guessing, but it's all I had.

I looked at the sun overhead. I had about three hours of good light left to find this guy and do something. The tracks seemed to thin out a little as I moved on. Maybe he'd started moving from rock to rock, like I'd been doing, here and there stepping on leaves only where they looked moist. Avoiding dry leaves and sticks, I moved up the hill and a little east. Here and there, I still found a bootprint to tell me I was on the trail.

I sensed I was getting close to the hideout and stayed low, moving slowly. Joanna might guess it was me down here, but I didn't want to draw any fire from her. I crouched beside a huge cedar tree, studying the ground above me. It was puzzling.

I saw tracks leading up along a bare slope—the tracks were pretty clear, but in places, they had been wiped out, like a heavy object had brushed over them. My eyes came to rest on a brownish-red spot and I studied it, looking for others. There were a few down at the bottom of the slope. Blood. I was pretty sure it was blood.

I studied the bare slope in front of me. A few large boulders topped it with a little space between them. There was a bare rock face in front of the boulders, maybe fifteen feet uphill.

I lifted my eyes to the ground above the rock face. Our hideout might be just above there. I couldn't be sure. When a rifle shot erupted from right above me, I turned and tucked myself behind the first boulder I could get to. That had come from that nest of boulders in front of the rock face. If he'd hoped to draw return fire from above, it hadn't worked. I grinned. Joanna was too smart to give away her position. Maybe, I thought, she was above him, waiting for a target to show up.

I studied the rock face above me. He almost had to be between the boulders and the rock face, probably snugged up against the wall. Then I had an idea. Mind you, I don't get a lot of really smart ideas, but I was pretty sure I had one now. I eased out from behind the boulder.

EIGHTEEN
CALL FOR HELP

He was up there, in between the rock face and the scattered boulders several feet in front of it. The tracks in front of me told me that. I kneeled beside the boulder I was using for cover. I was about thirty feet downhill and a bit to the side. I scanned the ground up ahead, looking for anything that would tip me off about where he was hiding. There was nothing I could see.

I knew Joanna didn't have a shot from above, and I was still counting on her being up there and watching for him. That just left me one thing to do. I needed to flush him out so one of us could get a shot.

Kneeling and sighting down the barrel of my Winchester, I steadied myself and aimed between two boulders for the middle of that rock wall. The bullet would come in from a slight angle, giving me some ricochet off the rock when it struck the face. I was counting on that.

I squeezed off the first shot and waited, watching

for what I could see between those boulders. There was no movement and no sound. At least, I thought, he must be a tad uncomfortable up there after that shot. I was sure he hadn't known I was down here before now.

I studied the layout up there again. I believed the hideout where Joanna had gone would be above the area where he'd hidden and on the far side of it. Good chance, I thought, that he had tucked himself away down on my end and against the protection of the rock face.

This time, I shifted my aim just slightly so the bullet would glance off the side of a boulder and ricochet back toward my end. I was hoping it would come in and strike that rock face behind another boulder that was blocking my view. That's where he was likely hiding.

I fired the second time and still saw no movement, but I was rewarded by the sound of a little cussin' going on up there. I sent another shot to the same place, holding just a little lower this time.

There was still nothing I could see, but a rifle shot boomed from up above, and now he pitched forward, landing on his stomach. I could just see the upper half of him lying still on the ground. I had driven him out and into Joanna's sights.

Not wanting to make any sudden moves, I put my hat on the end of my rifle, stood, and waved it in the air. I figgered if anybody else had come huntin' for us, they could shoot my hat and announce their presence. When I heard Joanna's voice calling from above, I put my hat back on and climbed up to take a look.

I didn't know him. I'd rolled him over on his back. Joanna's shot had taken him dead center, and he was gone. I had a feelin' the world wouldn't miss him much, but I didn't recognize him.

Hearing footsteps, I jumped to my feet, then relaxed when I saw Joanna rushing toward me. She gave me a hug and a kiss, then stepped back to look at the dead man. She turned away slightly. I wondered if she had ever killed a man before. It's not an easy thing.

"I don't know him," she said in a small voice.

"Me neither." I stepped back over to give her a hug again. "Is your horse up in the hideout?" I asked.

She nodded.

"Just bring him down and I'll take care of this," I said gently. "We can use your horse to get him to the bottom of the trail, and I'll see to it he gets a proper burial somewhere at the foot of the mountains."

She trotted away, probably glad to get away from this. I kneeled and took another look, then shook my head. I was sure I hadn't seen him before. I checked his pockets, but there was nothing there. Finally, I noticed something etched on his gun belt. I leaned down for a closer look and saw initials: IP.

"Ike Penfield," I mumbled to myself. It had to be him. I looked around me again, wondering if he'd come up here by himself. Maybe he'd seen Joanna and thought this would be an easy way to flush me out. Maybe, I thought, he sent some guys up to bring back the rest of his stash from Ice Lake. Sarge and Holt would have to be careful.

The clip-clop of hooves brought me back to my feet. I stood and took the reins to Joanna's horse. She still wasn't looking at him. "Ike Penfield, I'm pretty sure," I told her. "You did what you had to do."

She only nodded. I patted her shoulder. "You can start on down the trail," I said. "I'll load him on the horse and meet you down at the bottom."

A dead man is a heavy load. I knew that from my days of sheriffin' in Texas. I let out a holler when I gathered him up and heaved him over Joanna's horse. She didn't have any rope on the saddle, so I used the dead man's belt to tie his hands and feet together under the horse's belly, then started down the trail.

Luck smiled at me down at the bottom. Penfield's horse hadn't gone far. He trotted up when he saw us. I transferred Penfield to his own horse so Joanna could ride, then went to get my horse where I'd left him. We rode back to the ranch in silence, getting there just as darkness was falling.

I cut Penfield loose, tossed him in a trough, covered him with a tarp, and turned his horse loose in my corral. I would have to deal with him later.

━━━

Otis paused for only a moment when he reached the trail that branched off toward Lat Smith's ranch. He had been with Dugan and the miners for the two days before today, helping them divide the recovered gold diggings and then move the ore to safety.

Otis had hunkered down with Dugan, who was needed for several more days by the miners. They would have to plan for the safe transfer of ore in the future. They couldn't count on safe passage, even if this bunch of bandits had been knocked out. Otis had left them to make those plans. He had to get back.

Otis had already known he was going back first to help, that wasn't the question now. The only question was where he would be needed by the time he was at this exact branch on the road. Did he need to go back to Smith's ranch, or did he need to ride on into Silverton? Was he needed for scouting or for firepower?

He stopped just long enough to take a few good puffs on his cigar, then moved his horse forward on the trail into Silverton. Dugan had said something that made it easier to decide. He'd been thinking about it all day as he moved along this trail.

"Lat Smith, he's canny, and he's salty," Dugan had said. "I dunno if Sarge or Holt or anybody else is gonna be with him when you get there, but I'm bettin' he can hold down that ranch house or wherever he holes up. He kin hold it agin' Preacher an' whoever else Preacher's got. He'll need to know what's goin' on in town, though. If Preacher ain't bringin' the fight to Lat, then Lat will bring it to Preacher, an' he'll need to know what he's up against."

Otis glanced up at the sun overhead. He had a few hours yet before he hit town. He would get there before it got dark, but just before. That's what he wanted. He pulled down his hat and let his mouse-colored mustang eat up the miles.

Otis halted on the edge of town. He had a bad feeling, and he wasn't quite sure why. It was dusk—just about the time he'd wanted to get here. He had moved off the trail about a mile back, worried about sentries posted outside of town. Now poised to enter, he pulled back into the woods and edged closer to the livery stable, just now visible on his left.

Old Jackson at the livery stable was a friend, and Otis didn't worry about being betrayed by Jackson. It was the rest of the town he was worried about. He grinned and shook his head in the growing darkness. Maybe he was just turning into a nervous old lady for no reason.

Not willing to ignore that bad feeling in his gut, Otis dismounted and moved through the trees at the edge of town until he reached the alley behind the livery stable. There was a gate at the back leading inside. The hayloft was right above when anyone entered from the back, with stalls to both sides leading to the open corral area in the front.

Otis eased the back gate open and led the mustang inside. He could hear Jackson mucking out a stall to his left. Otis let his reins drop and moved to look inside the stall where he could hear the shoveling.

Jackson froze with a shovelful of manure half-lifted, staring at Otis. He lowered the shovel to the ground quietly and motioned for silence with his free hand. His eyes rose to look at the loft above them. Otis understood.

Jackson stepped out of the stall he was cleaning and tethered Otis's horse inside an empty stall, then slipped out the back, motioning for Otis to follow. He closed the back gate noiselessly before letting out a sigh of relief.

"Preacher's got that thug Blondie stationed in the loft with a rifle," Jackson murmured. "His gunhand Bert is staked out between the saloon and the general store most times, lookin' to put a bullet in you and several others. Preacher don't care nuthin' about a fair fight if either Penfield or Lat Smith comes back to town. He'll fight you straight up hisself, but he don't care nuthin' about how his boys get the job done no more." He stared at Otis. "Preacher wouldn't much mind puttin' you in a pine box, neither."

"Me!" Otis was only a little surprised. Preacher hadn't ever been too particular who he buried.

"Yep," Jackson nodded. "Word's done got out that you been heppin' Smith and Holt and Dugan and Sarge and them boys."

"Huh." Otis took off his hat and scratched his head. "He's fightin' against Penfield too? I thought them boys was in this together."

"Not no more." Jackson shook his head vigorously. "Them two had themselves what you would call a dis-a-gree-ment," he explained, drawing out the word and looking around nervously. "I think there's somebody you need to talk to while yore in town, though. I can take you to him and keep you safe."

Otis fell into step beside Jackson as they moved down the alley. Jackson paused and looked around the corner at each gap they came to. Otis shook his head, wondering what had happened to this town in a short week or two.

Jackson stopped behind Joanna's Bakery, tapped on the back door, then pushed it open quietly. They were met by a man holding a Colt .45. Otis was amazed to see it was the general store owner. He looked around the room, only dimly lit by one candle. He saw the feed store owner, the blacksmith, and the bank president, who stepped forward and asked Otis to take a seat.

Jackson stepped out the back. "Gotta go now," he said quietly.

"Rasmussen," the bank president said, shaking Otis's hand. "Word has it you've thrown in your hat with Latigo Smith, Sarge, and Holt?"

Surprised, Otis could only nod. They all stared at him, and he found his tongue. "That's right," he agreed. "Them others I was runnin' with was a bunch of snakes. I like the company better with these boys you jest said."

"Good." Rasmussen took a seat beside Otis. "The others haven't been seen around here. We've been hoping you would show up again. We need help from you boys. Especially from Latigo Smith. We gotta take this town back."

That was the first thing Otis had heard since he'd gotten to town that didn't surprise him. He looked around the circle of faces and waited.

"Preacher Dalton and Ike Penfield, between 'em, have taken over this town and they're bleeding us dry. They're killing the town," Rasmussen told him. There were murmurs of agreement from around the small kitchen area where they were meeting.

"I jest heard Dalton and Penfield don't get along so good anymore," Otis objected. "How can they both take it over?"

Rasmussen shrugged. "Each of 'em takes what he wants," the banker growled. "They haven't full-tilt started fighting with each other over who gets what, but they will. Meanwhile, we're all losing our shops and businesses. We're losing the whole town!"

Otis looked around the room again. He had a feeling he knew what they wanted, and it sounded dangerous. He licked his suddenly dry lips and leaned forward. "Who's the law in the town these days?" he asked. "I mean, I'm guessin' you boys want us to ride in here and take the town back."

"We do." Rasmussen sounded relieved. "Holt and Miss Joanna got their businesses taken. Ike Penfield took the bank from me. Some of these guys"—he swept an arm around the room—"are still open, but Preacher and his boys take whatever they want out of the cash boxes."

Otis waited for his question to be answered.

Rasmussen leaned in. "Preacher Dalton is the law right now," he said. "And that worthless brother-in-law of Penfield is the mayor, but they don't know we took a secret vote right here in this bakery the night before last. Knowles ain't the mayor anymore, he just don't know it. I'm the mayor. We'll support Latigo Smith as sheriff on anything he does. Even if he doesn't want to be sheriff, we'll support him to clean up this town. We need you to tell him."

These guys were serious, Otis could see that. He leaned back and stared at the table in front of him. "I don't have no idea a'tall if Lat Smith wants to be sheriff," he mumbled. He cleared his throat and looked at Rasmussen, whose face dropped.

"But," Otis went on. Rasmussen looked up hopefully. "I know he's gonna want Miss Joanna an' his friend Holt to get their businesses back. I'll help him for sure, an' I'll bet Sarge and Holt can't be kept outta this neither." He stopped and chuckled. "Probly Miss Joanna, too. I'll ride out and talk to them first thing in the mornin'."

Rasmussen thumped the table in satisfaction. He looked at the others in the room. "Maybe you boys all better get back to your shops," he said. "I'll stay and tell Otis everything I think they all need to know."

The others filed out the back door, patting Otis on the back or shaking his hand on the way out.

Otis spread his hands on the table. "I know about Blondie in the hayloft at the stable and my old partner Bert hidin' out in the alley back there," he said. "What else do I need to know afore we ride into town?"

━━

The sun was just breaking over the peaks when I sat on the porch, deciding what I had to do first today. Penfield, or whoever he was, hadn't moved from the trough where I had put him yesterday. I wasn't going to bury him around my house, but maybe I would take him out there near the mountains where he had died.

The town of Silverton was under somebody's heel. Maybe it had been Penfield. He was the smart one, but Preacher was the scary one. He could and did enforce things with his gun. That scared people. Preacher would be hard to get rid of.

That reminded me—I had meant to check the saddlebags of the dead man's horse to make sure it was Penfield I had shot yesterday. The initials on his belt made me think so, but I needed to be sure.

I set my coffee cup on the rail of the porch and walked out to the corral. The saddle and his bags were lying over the top rail of the corral. I reached into the saddlebags and started pulling things out. Five minutes later, everything was lying on the ground and I still didn't have any clues.

Joanna came out of the house and watched in silence while I went through the stuff on the ground one more time. Nothing. I shook my head and looked over at her. She had guessed what I was doing.

"He doesn't have anything that tells me that was really Penfield," I mumbled. "Nothing in his pockets, nothing in the bags..." My voice trailed off. I knew I needed to tell her she'd been right about the things we had argued about last night.

I walked over to put my arms around her waist. "You're right—what we talked about last night. I can't just ride into town by myself and clean up Silverton. Too many guns against me there. I'll have to wait for help."

Joanna heaved a sigh of relief and rested her head against my shoulder. "How much help?" she asked. "How many people do you need? We don't know what things are like in town right now. A lot could have changed."

I shrugged and nodded at the same time, staring over her shoulder. Suddenly, I pulled back and pointed. People were moving across the pasture out there, headed for the house. Three of them, it looked like, with maybe two mules or horses behind them.

I couldn't tell who it was, so I trotted to the house for my binoculars. Joanna waited, watching me. I broke into a grin. "Looks like Sarge and Holt," I burst out, "and they've maybe got themselves some loot and a prisoner. Looks like I've got some help, just in time."

We waited by the corral, watching them ride on in. "I've seen that prisoner," Joanna said. "He was in the bakery a time or two. Maybe he can tell us if that was really Penfield after us yesterday."

We gave each other a couple slaps on the back when they reached the corral. The prisoner sat on his horse, glaring at everybody. "Who is Sunshine over there?" I asked. "One of the robbers, I know, but what's his name?"

He spoke for the first time. "Deuce," he snarled. He stared at me. "Penfield knows where you live," he reminded me. "He'll be back."

"That's too bad," I said. "I was thinking maybe you were too much trouble and I would just cut you loose if you disappear and never come back."

He just stared at me. "Of course," I told him. "If you decide to do some more robbing, you'll wind up as dead as some of your buddies out there."

He shook his head slowly. "I'm gonna be a dead man, either way," he moaned. "Penfield won't let me live if I cross him." He stared at the ground. "That there is a hard man. I'd rather cross you than cross him."

"You can do me a favor," I told him, walking over to the trough and pulling back the tarp. "Tell me if you know who this is. Who it was, I mean."

Deuce walked over and stared into the trough. He

nodded and came over to me, holding out his wrists. "That's Penfield," he confirmed. He held out his wrists, tied together by a thick rope. "You cut me loose an' you won't never see me again," he promised. "Californy sounds real good right now. I got me a sister out there."

Three minutes later, he was just a cloud of dust, riding due west. The others were looking at me funny. "We got no place to hold him," I pointed out. "No jail to put him in. We ain't even legal if we tie him up and hold him in the root cellar." One by one, they all nodded. I grabbed a shovel and Sarge went out to the tool shed for another. An hour later, we had planted Penfield at the foot of the mountains.

NINETEEN
TAKING THE TOWN

"I s there any chance we can all live with Preacher Dalton actin' like the sheriff in Silverton?" I was pretty sure I knew the answer, but I had to ask. They all shook their heads, even Joanna.

We were hunched over a hand-drawn map of the town, which I had spread out on the table. Sarge had marked everything he could remember, which was most things. The trail to town from here took us to the livery stable first. Moving down Greene Street, there was the general store, blacksmith, bank, Suds 'n Such, and Joanna's Bakery. A few other shops ran along for a few blocks, then the barber shop and undertaker were the same shop, down at the far end.

Sarge pointed at the Suds 'n Such. "Ain't no way we can come in there after him," Sarge declared. "He can get all forted up in there, even if we come in the back door. Somebody'll shoot us in the back for sure."

I stared at the rest of the map. "He could have folks

posted in other places, too," I pointed out in frustration. "Can I just come into town without getting' shot at from who knows where?"

Everybody shook their heads and stared at the map. Joanna's lips were drawn down into a thin line. She kept looking up at me. I wondered if maybe it would just be best to wait and see if Preacher came after us out here. Meanwhile, though, Holt and Joanna would still be locked out of their businesses. And who knew what else was going on in town?

Hoofbeats sounded outside. Joanna got up and dashed over to the window, standing to the side and looking out. "Otis!" she said. I could hear the relief in her voice at seeing it was a friend. That told me one thing I needed to know—we couldn't just stay holed up out here and wait for Preacher Dalton to come to us. The waiting would be too hard for us. I would have to take the fight to him.

Otis came through the door, spied the map on the table, and pulled up a chair for himself. "I just been to town," he announced. "I kin tell you boys whatever you need to know." A frown appeared on his face for an instant. "Excep' for Ike Penfield," he added. "I don't know what's become of Penfield. Nobody over there to the town knew what he's up to."

"We just got done buryin' Penfield," Sarge told him. "Tell us what you know about Silverton. Preacher having his way there?"

"Yep." Otis pulled the map over and pointed at the livery stable. "He's got that muscle man Blondie posted up there in the hayloft, waitin' to take a potshot at you boys when you ride in." Then he pointed at the saloon and general store on the map. "My old partner, Bert, is waitin' in the alley between them two stores, ready to dry-gulch somebody if he can." His lips curled in a sneer.

Otis told me he'd met with the store owners and bank president in the back of the bakery, and he told me how Rasmussen would back me, him being the mayor, if I came to town and took down Preacher Dalton. I looked up from the map to catch Joanna's eye. She was a little pale, but she caught my eye and nodded.

"Do what you have to do, Lat," she said.

I took a deep breath, studied the map, and told everybody where I wanted them.

"Otis, you go in first," I told him. "Take down Blondie in the livery stable and you get up there yourself. If Preacher has any more dry-gulchers riding into town, you can, uh…read to them from the good book and show them the error of their ways." Otis grinned.

"Sarge," I said, looking at him next. "I need you to catfoot around behind Bert and take him outta the picture before I get that far down the street. Holt," I said, swinging around to him, "come in from the other side of town and make sure this is a fair fight from your end."

"What about me?" All eyes swung to Joanna.

I should have known she wouldn't let me leave her out of this. I reached out to take her hand.

"I'm going to wait at the edge of town for thirty minutes," I said. "I need you to ride to the livery and make sure Otis is ready to go there at the livery before I come in. Even Preacher and his boys aren't low enough to shoot at a woman. You can come back and give me the word when it's clear for me to ride in."

I looked around the room. "Everybody good with this?" I asked.

Everybody nodded, and I stood. "Let's go get 'em," I said.

◻

Otis stood poised on the top rung of the ladder into the hayloft, peering over the edge. Blondie had dragged a hay bale over and was seated at the edge, rifle cradled across his arms. Jackson, the livery stable guy, had told Otis this was what he could expect. Otis checked the ground between here and Blondie—he couldn't get there in a rush unless Blondie got distracted. That's where old Jackson came into the picture.

Otis hefted a long, thick chunk of wood in one hand and his other hand rested on his pistol. He would rather use the wood, but he would shoot if Blondie gave him no choice. Otis narrowed his eyes and stared across the loft. Blondie's head slipped a little to one side, then came back up. Was he napping? Otis barely dared to hope he was that lucky.

Down below, there was a sudden, jarringly loud clang. Blondie's head snapped up and he half-rose out of his chair.

"Whaddya doin' down there, old-timer?" he

bellowed. "Sounds like a train goin' off the rails." Blondie took a seat again but kept glaring down into the stable.

"Sorry," Jackson mumbled. "Dropped the shovel, that's all."

"What didya drop it on? An iron stove?" Blondie continued to stare down at Jackson. Too late, he heard the footsteps rushing up behind him.

Blondie lifted his rifle and swung it up as he turned to face his attacker, but he was too late. Otis swung the wood through the air and heard a satisfying *thunk!* as he connected with the side of Blondie's head.

Blondie fell sideways, landing face down in the hay. He didn't move. Otis dropped the wood and yanked Blondie's belt off, using it to tie his hands behind him. In a moment, Jackson had climbed the ladder and he handed Otis a length of rope, which Otis used to tie the feet together.

Blondie weighed over two hundred pounds, but Otis managed to drag him down the ladder with a little help from Jackson. They stuffed a bandanna into his mouth and dragged him into an empty stall.

Otis heaved a deep breath and looked at Jackson. "Miss Joanna and Lat Smith are waiting to hear we've taken care of Blondie," he said.

Jackson dragged his sleeve across his forehead to mop off the sweat. He nodded with satisfaction. "I'll go and tell Miss Joanna she can come down here," he told Otis.

———

Down the street about fifty yards, Sarge peeked around the corner of the general store. Bert was lounging against the side of the building. He had a rifle propped against the wall next to him. He wore tied-down guns on both hips.

Sarge stayed where he was, watching for a full two minutes. He needed to give Otis a little time. They were counting on Otis getting his job done quietly. That would allow Lat to get into town without drawing fire. If Sarge had to shoot Bert, well, that would alert Preacher, but Lat could still come in and have a fair, one-on-one fight.

When two minutes had passed, Sarge eased forward noiselessly. This, he thought, wasn't really that hard. The dry, packed dirt in front of him had no sticks or dry leaves to alert Bert to his presence. Anyway, Bert was staring straight ahead, not expecting an attack from behind.

When he was just two steps away, Sarge pulled his Colt from the holster and reversed his grip, grabbing it by the barrel. Bert heard the whisper of noise. He reached down to pull the right-hand gun, ducked, and whirled toward the noise. He saw only Sarge's boots before he blacked out. Sarge grabbed him under both arms and dragged him back to the alley behind the general store. The store owner was only too happy to help tie him up.

Down at the far end of town, Holt stayed on his horse and sized things up before riding in. Most of the action, he knew, would be down at the other end of the street. He saw only two down-at-the-heels drifters sitting in front of the barbershop. Both wore guns. One was sipping something from a flask.

Holt studied them for a minute before riding in. He didn't know if they were trouble or not, but he couldn't take the chance. The one sipping from the flask especially—who knew if he would decide to chip in on a gunfight?

Holt tied up his horse on the rail in front of the barbershop, then lifted his shotgun from the saddle. He turned casually, pointing the shotgun at the ground in front of their feet.

"What are you boys doin' in town?" he drawled.

The guy with the flask drew back his lips into a snarl, showing some yellow teeth. "What bizness is it of your'n?" he growled.

Holt lifted the shotgun slightly so it covered them both from a distance of only five yards. Both stared at the double barrels, then at Holt.

"Well, now," Holt drawled. "Mebbe you're right. Mebbe it ain't none of my business. Here's the thing, though. Things are about to get mighty lively in this town. I expect somebody's gonna get planted up at Boot Hill today. You boys can join 'em if you want to. Otherwise, I think you need to straddle them broncs and ride out of town."

They stared at each other, saying nothing. The one with the flask tucked it away in his pocket, then both stood, walked over to their horses, and rode out of town.

Sitting on our horses in the shade of the trail near the edge of town, Joanna and I waited. I couldn't remember time ever going by this slowly. I pulled the watch she had given me from my pocket and looked at it again. Joanna smiled slightly and shook her head.

"I think it's only been about two minutes since you checked it last time," she told me. Her face was drawn with the tension. I guess maybe mine was, too.

We had agreed I would wait here for thirty minutes to let Otis, Sarge, and Holt button up the town before I rode in to have it out with Preacher Dalton. Only ten minutes had gone by so far. It felt like it should be dinner time already.

Finally, we heard some rustling off to our right, away from the trail. That would almost certainly be Otis or Jackson, coming to bring Joanna to the stable, but you just can't be too careful. My hand rested on the top of my Colt until Jackson emerged from the trees and waved to us.

Joanna leaned over to give me a kiss, dismounted, and followed Jackson on foot. Now I waited alone.

I waited for as long as I could stand it before I pulled the watch from my pocket again. Ten minutes to go. I couldn't just sit here any longer. I dismounted, tethered my horse to a tree, and walked in small circles, swinging my arms. Then I stood quietly beside my horse, letting the tension drain away while I thought about the ranch and my future with Joanna. When I checked the watch again, it was time to go. I looked up to see Joanna waving at me from the edge of town.

We had talked about this long into the night last night. Preacher would try to give himself any advantage he could, and I couldn't give him any. The main street ran north-south, so there wouldn't be any direct sun in my eyes either way. Still, I couldn't let him face me across the street with the morning sun in my eyes.

He probably had spies on the lookout for me in town. Not just for me, but for Penfield, since he didn't know Penfield was dead. Holt and Sarge, too. He would look for them. I had decided to tip off his spies on purpose. No use in putting things off when I got to town. The most likely places he would have people on the lookout would be at the train station and at the café. Those two places weren't very far apart.

I tethered my horse at the rail outside the train station. I would take it on foot from here. When I stepped into the station and stopped to look at a list of departing times, I saw a skinny kid dart out the back door.

Waiting just a minute or two, I started down toward the café. I didn't know if I would wait in there or not. As it turned out, I guess Preacher wanted to get this over with as much as I did.

He stepped out of the Suds 'n Such. The morning sun was at my back. He stepped out toward the middle of the street, so I did, too. They had told me he liked to fire off a lot of shots as fast as he could. Lightning-quick, they said. I wasn't that fast.

There were three things I was thinking about. I had

to draw steady and make the first shot count. I had to aim for the center of his body. And I had to watch his eyes. The eyes, they say, give it away when he's going for his gun. I had learned all of those things the hard way down in Texas.

He stopped in the middle of the street and gave me a wolfish-looking grin. "You could ride out of town and we could forget all this," he said. "My beef is with Penfield, anyway. You don't owe me nuthin'."

I shook my head. "I don't think so," I said. "Penfield is dead. Besides, you want too much. We'd be buttin' heads sooner or later."

The surprise at hearing about Penfield flashed for just a second. Then a mask seemed to drop over his face. He angled his head toward the Suds 'n Such. "Is it 'cause I taken the saloon away from your friend?"

His eyes flashed, and I knew he'd tried to throw me off with the talking. My hand swept down for my gun as his first shot exploded past my ear. I leveled and fired. That shot took him in the belly and he staggered back, but the gun was coming up again. It roared, and I felt a blow strike me in the leg.

I fell to one knee, and that might have saved my life. His next shot went high. I fired twice and sent both shots into his chest. He sunk to his knees and dropped his gun, staring at me. His mouth worked up and down like he was tryin' to say something, then he fell forward on his face.

Things went a little fuzzy there for a while. Sarge came runnin' out from between two buildings, holding his gun out and tellin' folks to back away from me. Otis came out from the livery stable, then

Joanna ran past him and sank to her knees in front of me. Things swam around, and I fell forward into her...

———

The next thing I knew, I was in a bed with some kind of contraption holding my leg up in the air. Joanna was sitting next to me, and I remember those beautiful eyes lighting up when she saw me try to sit up. I didn't have time to ask her anything before the doctor came stumping into the room.

"What's goin' on, doc?" I asked. I pointed at the contraption holding my leg up. "How come my leg's stickin' up in the air like that?"

"On account you've got a hole in your leg," he barked.

I slumped back against my pillow. "Well, thanks for breakin' it to me gentle, doc," I whined.

He shook his head. "Ornery patients, that all I get is ornery patients," he muttered. He pointed at the leg. "Bullet went through clean. You'll be fine if you keep still for a while and don't get yourself shot again." He pointed at Joanna. "Keep him quiet," he ordered.

Joanna chuckled. "You heard him," she told me. "You have to keep quiet and do what I tell you."

"That's not exactly what he said," I protested, but she smothered my objections with a kiss. That wasn't too bad, I had to admit.

We got interrupted when Sarge and Holt walked in and started doin' a lot of harrumphing. Joanna gave me a pat and stood. "I'll be back in a little bit," she said. "Is there anything you want me to get?"

"Just one thing," I said. "Tell Fred down at the general store that I need to see him." She looked puzzled but nodded and left.

Sarge and Holt looked at me, then at the leg. "Gonna be okay," I told them. "Doc says the bullet went right through." I looked around as Otis came through the door. "Is Preacher dead?" I asked. "Things got a little fuzzy there."

"Dead as Caesar," Holt nodded. "And we sent his boys packin' already. Bert and Blondie, they're gone. They taken a train outta here a half hour ago. Bert, he objected some, but Otis over here explained he didn't have no choice."

Otis grinned and massaged his fist. "My old partner," Otis mumbled. "He just chose the wrong side, that's all."

Somewhere along the way, I guess I drifted off to sleep. When I woke up, Fred from the general store was walking through the door. He moved over to stand by the bed.

"Joanna said you need to see me," he said. "You just tell me what you need. Silverton is gonna be a wonderful town again, thanks to you."

"Well, I don't know about that," I mumbled. He waved his hands in the air. "Okay," I said, "I'm wondering if you have any rings."

His forehead scrunched up. "What kind of rings?" he asked. "I've got a couple..." Then it dawned on him. "Oh! You want a ring for your lady friend. You're thinkin' about goin' to a sky pilot and all that stuff." He grinned. "I don't have anything right now, but with the train runnin' through town these days, I can get something in right away. You just come on down to the store when you can and we'll talk about it."

I was trying to stay awake until Joanna came back, but I guess I hadn't had much sleep lately. My eyelids got real heavy, and somewhere along the way, I just dozed off again.

TWENTY
PLANS MADE

SIX WEEKS LATER

I t had taken two trips to the old abandoned mine at Ice Lake to get the rest of the diggings stolen from the miners. I hadn't been much help. I'd made the first trip with them, but they had done all the hauling while I hopped along on a cane. The leg had gotten *all swole up* after the days of riding, as Sarge said, so I had stayed home on the second trip. Joanna was a lot happier with that choice.

The miners had wanted to give me a reward, but I hadn't let them. They had promised Holt a lot of business at the Suds 'n Such, and the whole town was happy to have Holt running that place again. The miners, well, they gave that place a lot of business as it was, but now they had more money to drop there at the saloon. Holt was happy.

Joanna was back in business, too. I'd told the miners to stop in there as a reward to me, but I think they would have, anyway. They couldn't get enough of stuffing their faces with pies and cakes and such.

Sarge, well, Sarge was a man who just didn't need much. He helped out Holt at the saloon, and he would help me too once I got the ranch up and running.

Speaking of the ranch, it looked like I could get the place going now that things had settled down. I had a little money put by to get a herd started, plus Jed had left a few cows behind when he moved. I just had to get some cows and fix a few things up around the place.

Things were peaceful now, that was the main thing. Penfield, Preacher, and that lot were either in the ground or moved out. Folks talked some at the saloon about Brown's Hole, out there in Utah, and how there were some horse thieves and outlaws, but that was a long way from here. I had done enough to keep the peace, that's the way I saw it.

Rasmussen and some other shopkeepers had come to me and asked about being the sheriff, but I had turned them down. Just a rancher now, I told them. I was sure they could find somebody good, and I would help the new guy a little if he needed me. That's the way we'd left it.

I was settled on the back porch of the house right now, with Joanna bringing me food and coffee and telling me to stay off my bad leg. Truth is, the leg was almost healed, but I liked the attention. Plus, I had a ring in the dresser back there in the bedroom. I wasn't sure whether I wanted to get it now or wait until she came out to the ranch after closing the bakery for the day later on.

All of a sudden, we heard a lot of mooing and commotion. It was on the trail to town, that's where the noise was. Joanna and I stared at each other. I got up and hobbled off the porch, staring down the trail. Through the dust, I could see a herd of cows, and the guy up front was so big it had to be Dugan.

"Gotcha some cows, we did," he boomed when he got a little closer to me. I stared behind him. Sarge and Holt were back there, driving maybe fifty cows into my place. I watched while Holt opened the gate and they drove the herd in.

Dugan dismounted, walked past me, and plopped down in a chair on the porch. The chair squeaked a few times, but it didn't collapse. Dugan was grinning at me. "I know you didn't want no reward," he boomed, "but me and a few of the boys didn't think that was right. We're still up there in them hills, bringin' in some good color on account of you."

He waved his hand at the pasture where the cows he had brought had joined the few left behind by Jed. They milled around out there for a bit, then they spread out and grazed. I have to admit, it was a pleasant sight.

"Like you said, I didn't want a reward," I pointed out.

Dugan waved his arms around again. "Well, here's the thing, Lat. You've got fifty-six new cows on your pasture, and we ain't gonna drive 'em out again." He looked around at Sarge and Holt, who had joined us on the porch. They nodded.

Dugan took a huge slurp from the cup of coffee

Joanna had brought him and tipped his hat at her. He set the cup down and stood. "Well," he said, "I've got me some panning to do, so I can't set around here jawin' with you boys all day." He mounted up, waved, and rode out.

Holt took the chair Dugan had just given up while Sarge settled himself on the porch rail. Holt grinned. "It was my idea," he admitted. "Some of the boys were chewing things over at the saloon last night, and we came up with this." He sat back, very pleased with himself.

I looked over at Sarge. "What about you?" I asked. "They must have done something for you."

Sarge stared down at his boots. Holt just sat back and waited for Sarge to talk. I could tell something was up. "Well, the thing is," Sarge mumbled, "You didn't want that sheriffin' job, and I been in the army and such. The boys decided mebbe I could help the town…" He pulled back his vest and showed me the badge on his chest.

I chuckled and stood up to shake his hand. "Good man for the job," I agreed. I stared out at the cows, wondering who would help me now.

Sarge and Holt looked at each other. Holt cleared his throat. "Otis ain't done no cowboyin', but he could learn, and he needs sumthin'," Holt began.

"He's welcome out here," I interrupted. "He saved my hide a time or two. I'm sure I can teach him anything he needs to know."

Holt and Sarge mounted up and rode away. Joanna came over to sit on my lap. "Everything worked out great, didn't it?" she murmured in my ear. She kissed my forehead and stood. "Got to open up the shop," she told me.

"Hold on." I moved past her and into the bedroom, where the dresser stood with the ring in it. I had gotten it from Fred at the general store just the other day. Joanna wrapped her arms around me the minute she saw me coming with the box.

"Yes!" she said, kissing me on the ear. "Yes!"

"I haven't asked anything yet," I protested, struggling to get down on one knee.

Joanna waved her hands in the air. "Okay, so ask!" she said impatiently. She pulled me back up. "Don't hurt your leg, Lat."

I chuckled and stood. I can't remember exactly the words I found to say. They seemed to come out a little jumbled up, but then again, I already had the answer. It was still Yes.

Now, I thought, I've got my chance. I'd come from Texas to Colorado to find a life for myself, to have a chance at the things I wanted. Sometimes, it seems like if you keep working at a thing, it can all turn out right.

A LOOK AT BOOK THREE
LATIGO'S TROUBLE: MELTDOWN IN LEADVILLE

In the rugged Colorado high country of the 1880s, Latigo Smith is bracing for the toughest battle of his life.

Ready to settle down with his bride on a tranquil ranch, Latigo envisions a peaceful future amid the region's booming gold and silver strikes. But danger lurks with outlaws and opportunists running rampant.

When old friend Marshall Bart Anderson arrives from the lawless boomtown of Leadville, overwhelmed by its widespread crime, he pleads for Latigo's help. Torn between his desire for a peaceful life and a sense of duty to his friend, Latigo finds himself drawn back into the fray.

After outlaws steal his horses and menace his new home, he faces an agonizing choice: stand by and hope for peace or risk it all to protect his friend and his future. As tensions mount, Latigo must confront a truth he can't ignore—some battles are forged in the heart, and victory demands more than courage.

AVAILABLE DECEMBER 2024

ABOUT THE AUTHOR

Patrick Lindsay came to Texas by way of Missouri, Canada, and California and has been proud to call the Lone Star State his home for more than forty years now. He retired in 2017 from "another life" as a CPA, whereafter he turned his hand to writing.

He has read just about everything by Louis L'Amour and first decided to give Western writing a try on his initial day of retirement. He has been writing ever since and loves the idea that so many people get enjoyment from his work.

Patrick and his wife Michelle live on a cattle ranch near Fort Worth along with cows, horses, chickens, and a very spoiled Great Pyrenees dog. He is an avid fan of the St. Louis Cardinals in baseball and the Kansas City Chiefs in football.